Swan Town

Swan Town

The Secret Journal of
Susanna Shakespeare

Michael J. Ortiz

HarperCollins*Publishers*

Special thanks to Tara Weikum and Laura Strachan

Library of Congress Cataloging-in-Publication Data
Ortiz, Michael J.
    Swan Town : the secret journal of Susanna Shakespeare /
Michael J. Ortiz.—1st ed.
        p. cm.
    Summary: Restricted by the authorities from practicing
Catholicism and forbidden by her parents from seeing a Puritan boy,
Susanna, the daughter of William Shakespeare, vents her anger by
writing in a journal and composing a play.
    ISBN-10: 0-06-058126-3 (trade : alk. paper) — ISBN-13: 978-0-06-
058126-8 (trade : alk. paper)
    ISBN-10: 0-06-058127-1 (lib. bdg. : alk. paper) — ISBN-13: 978-0-
06-058127-5 (lib. bdg. : alk. paper)
    1. Hall, Susanna Shakespeare, 1583–1649—Childhood and
youth—Juvenile fiction. 2. Shakespeare, William, 1564–1616—Juvenile
fiction. [1. Hall, Susanna Shakespeare, 1583–1649—Childhood and
youth—Fiction. 2. Shakespeare, William, 1564–1616—Fiction. 3.
Persecution—Fiction. 4. Diaries—Fiction. 5. Great Britain—History—
Elizabeth, 1558–1603—Fiction.] I. Title.
PZ7.O763Swa 2006
[Fic]—dc22   2005005729
                                                         CIP
                                                          AC

Typography by R. Hult
1 2 3 4 5 6 7 8 9 10

First Edition

For Kathleen

Swan Town

One

"... these ragged players ..."

Stratford, March 2, 1597. Where should I start? My hair is exactly the color of wet hay. My years on this earth are thirteen and three quarters. My fingers are slender. They like the feel of a quill's feathered strength. I even like the smell of ink. Mother says it reminds her of a piss pot, but that's just her sour side showing. Besides, O excellent piece of witchcraft, I believe this ink of mine actually keeps the flies away. Who would guess there could be such magic in a simple swan's feather? Yet maybe I shouldn't be too surprised. Have you ever looked a swan in the eye? There's a shiny black inkpot that will never run dry, I can tell you.

The idea of writing a journal came to me the other morning while I was chopping away at sheaves of rosemary in the kitchen. Its clean smell filled the house. Rosemary, as everyone knows, is for remembrance, for memory. So is this journal. A gathering of my days, before they fly who knows where. As Father would say, something forgotten is something lost.

Stratford, March 3, 1597. I live in a wonderful house, one with plenty of secret rooms and passages. The house and its leather shop really belong to my grandparents, though my family and I have lived here with them since I can remember.

My family except for my father, that is.

He is a player and poet who lives in London most of the year. His name is William, though he's most often called Will, and he's very popular among the playhouses on Bankside. Groundlings flock to see his fools and villains. Even the royal court has shown its favor to Father's troupe, the Lord Chamberlain's Men. They are the star in Her Majesty's Christmas revels.

At home, there is my mother, Anne, a strong-willed woman if there ever was one. I don't take after her, despite what people say. Well, maybe just a bit. And then there is Judith and her twin, Hamnet. They're eleven years old, and full of fun most of the time. And what would we do without uncles Gilbert and Richard? Their handcrafted leather is softer than a dog's ear, and they can turn a goat into a glove faster than any man in Stratford. They had better, because more foul-smelling skins of goats, sheep, deer, and cows come through here than I could ever count.

As I mentioned, my grandparents own this house. Grandfather remembers more about this town's history than anyone I know. Years ago he used to be high bailiff. These days he just works in his shop and sits by the fire with Grandmother, his sweetheart still.

Lastly, there's Uncle Edmund, who's only three years older than me and already wants to join the players in London like my father. Edmund and I have much in common, I think, though that's not something I go about telling everyone. I am a girl, after all, which in this town means I'm little more than a beast of burden, a slave to the spinning wheel for what seems like forever. I suspect Edmund won't remain in Stratford for very long. His mind ranges far and wide, and he has hopes as brave as my father's. Even though Edmund *can* be a little bossy at times, we are very close, and I love him dearly. Still, his talk of going to London has got me thrilled to the bone, and not a little bit jealous.

London. Home of bloodthirsty knaves and scapegraces. Switches and spurs! Edmund better be careful.

Stratford, March 4, 1597. Rain all day. Great sheets of it, washing the streets, swelling the river. In the morning I saved a field mouse from drowning. He's under my bed, in a box of warm straw. His name is Hubert.

Stratford, March 5, 1597. This morning, while clearing the dung from the front of our house, Uncle Edmund was practicing some of his speeches again. Kill'n' the calf, as Mother says. The muck hill's steam rose upward, a foul-smelling ghost. Market days always bring more horses, and hence more dung, more ghosts for Edmund to push away. Looking out my window, I could see him crunching the bugs that escaped his shovel and were scrambling across his stage. His dreams are the gold that will deliver him from this dusty town.

What will deliver me? Here in Stratford, sons follow their

fathers, year after year: Blacksmiths beget blacksmiths, cobblers beget cobblers, and women and girls bring harvest after harvest to kitchen day after day. Stubborn carbuncles! That's what I think of town traditions! A girl like me, more nimble of mind than finger, what am I to do? Hide my wit in a halfpenny purse and smile all day long? Someday, I hope, my father shall turn about in a London lane and perhaps, though I have, as of yet, no idea how, see his own daughter, free at last of country towns and their hidebound ways.

Stratford, March 6, 1597. Mother told me this afternoon that she thinks my journal writing a foolish thing. She says I'm gathering evidence for the prosecution. What times we live in, she says. Any other religion than the queen's is considered treasonous. Catholics are imprisoned. Consciences enchained. Even offering a priest food and shelter could put us in jail.

We go to the Trinity Church for established services, to not raise suspicions, but most of my family secretly practices the old faith, or at least the adults do. Children have to wait until they are old enough to understand such risks. I hope to join my family soon. It will be a pleasure to listen to something other than the marble-hearted villains at Trinity week after week. Their glare is pure wormwood to me.

But for now, I have to do something, or this silly patch of a town will turn me into a good-for-nothing lackwit. There's something about writing down my secret, innermost thoughts that makes all this spying and hiding about at least more bearable. I only pray that my journal does not convict me for a fool or a coward. Or land me in prison.

Anyhow, Sir Colin Hill, the official who makes sure our town prays according to Her Majesty's wishes, will never find this journal, so secretly have I hidden it. Grandfather has carved a secret drawer inside my writing desk. There my journal hides from the eyes of the world. And my family! I also have two or three quills and, next to them, sheets of paper smooth as a drift of snow, waiting for the next blast from my feverish brain.

If Sir Colin thinks he's doing God's work, he's cracked. He hunts down Catholics as if they were nothing more than half-bred English with no right to be in this kingdom, none at all. My family has been Catholic since long before I was born. I feel these ties to the old faith deeply. How could it make me a traitor when its teachings are a summons for me to love my neighbor as myself?

But enough. Such thoughts make my head grow sore, as if one of the vises in our shop were twisting tight at my temples! Take flight, you worries that make me shiver with fear.

Stratford, March 7, 1597. We all are vigilant these days. The quarter moon hangs like a sharp blade over the sky. Sir Colin has ordered three houses, not two streets down from us, searched for popish prayer books. Mother tells me to come away from the window. Our prayers are whispers.

Stratford, March 8, 1597. Received word from Father today. He says that he wants my uncles to visit him in London. They aren't wasting any time, either. Edmund and the rest of them depart this afternoon. Father's company of players needs some of our finest Warwickshire leather for their jerkins, gloves, boots, and other costumes for the stage. Why can't I go too? Next time, I swear. Other news: In London, near Bankside, by the royal barge, Father says a new theater has gone up, called the Swan. A perfect name for a theater, I think.

Stratford, March 9, 1597. Our fields and meadows have become a sea of daffodils, open at the first touch of spring. Would that I could sail over them to far-off islands, a kingdom of Aprils always golden with sun.

Stratford, March 10, 1597. Grandmother told me she thinks it strange that a girl would write as much as I do. Mother gave me a look that told me not to argue. What good would it do? I am lucky everyone else in the house but the two of them understands, or just ignores, my journal. And Grandmother's heart is as sweet as a raisin. She means well. But write I must.

Who would think that in a land where the queen can write half a dozen languages, women would be kept from books? Only boys get to go to school. I wish I could go, even though Hamnet thinks school boring and dislikes his petty master and the ironbound rules of Latin. Knavish boy! To sit at my own desk in a real classroom, with a hornbook all my own, gathering words like a swallow building a nest for the storms of life to come. How wonderful!

Let the narrow-minded banish us from the schoolroom. Here in my room I can write and read well enough. A girl who can read is like a bird with feathers as powerful as they are beautiful. Her wings are the pages of her book. No wall can imprison her.

Stratford, March 11, 1597. Grandfather and I went down to the river to look for swan feathers lying about. He showed me how to make my own quills using them. It's not so difficult, really. Feathers from the left wing of a swan are for the right-handed, and those from the right wing for the left-handed (that would be me). It has to do with the curve of the plumage. Once you've selected your feathers, you need to soak them in water awhile and then stick them into hot sand to harden their tips. The cutting of a nib is the challenging part. Your knife must be sharp, and your hand steady. And that's *before* you dip into your inkpot!

I love writing with something that has touched the sky.

Stratford, March 12, 1597. Mother still frowns on my keeping a journal but has not forbidden it. She wonders how I will have time to write and do all my housework. Fut! And so do I! The list is long. Judith and I must make soap, bread, tallow, butter, mustard with the quern, and malt and beer by the barrel with Grandfather and Hamnet. That is, when Grandfather's not asking for help in the shop with cutting and sewing. The orchards and gardens alone take hours to tend and harvest. And the dreary linen wheel (vile thief of time!) never stops spinning.

Stratford, March 13, 1597. Judith and I have decided to change the name of Stratford to Swan Town. The old name is simply not descriptive enough. We shall draw up the new town charter as soon as we get signatures from all the river's winged citizens.

Let me describe Swan Town for the benefit of anyone reading this journal years from now. Grandfather assures me that within the parish of Swan Town today live about 2,500 souls.

Between Mill Bridge and Clopton Bridge the River Avon runs like an arm slightly bent at the elbow. The surrounding fields on the edge of town are bordered by hundreds of sturdy elms.

The town streets are in the shape of a wobbly box. Henley Street, where I live, is to the north and Sanctuary Lane to the south. Clopton Bridge turns into Henley Street as soon as you walk past our two most popular taverns, the Swan and the Bear. For obvious reasons I favor the Swan. Though I've never been in either one!

Stratford, March 19, 1597. My uncles returned today after visiting in London with Father for three days. He's now living in Southwark, near the Rose theater, in the top floor of an old two-story house.

He looks well, says Edmund. Though his hair is thinning and his rheumy eyes show how hard he works, his kind ways are the same as ever. Father said he could still smell Grandfather's shop on the uncles, that bittersweet aroma of cowhide and sheepskin, which he swears will make us all outlive doomsday. A tanner's work is never undone, he joked.

On their last afternoon in London, they watched Father's play *Titus Andronicus* at the Swan, south of the river. Even sitting in the gallery, they found the smoke, the stench from the groundlings, and the stale smell of bitter ale began to annoy them before the play was half over. And Gilbert said that the seats, though well made, quickly grew uncomfortable.

But the play itself! Bloody deeds, carnal lusts, as many crimes as there were words spoken. Needless to say, we are all proud of Father beyond measure. I must get Edmund to tell me more when we have time alone, out of Mother's sight. She doesn't think playhouses fit subject for girls my age. Fie!

Stratford, March 20, 1597. Uncle Edmund showed me a clever stage trick today, one he learned in London. He took a fresh sheep's bladder he bought from the market, filled it with sheep's blood, and tucked it under his arm. When Judith walked in, he yelled out that life was too much to endure, fell on his sword, and squeezed his arm against his side so that the bright blood spurted out of his chest, spattering against the windows and walls. Judith nearly fainted with fright! Mooncalf! Only Hamnet managed to get her smiling again, and that took some time.

Stratford, March 21, 1597. Just when Judith and I were about to enjoy a morning all to ourselves while everyone was at market, Edmund decided to stay, to keep us company, he cheerily said. Even though Judith rolled her eyes (she finds Edmund a bit too adventurous for his own good, which of course is why I like him so much), I knew that this was a perfect opportunity to hear more about his trip to London.

Edmund followed me into the main room, by a low fire. Judith went upstairs. I could hear her singing a tune about a swan that died for love.

"So you must tell me everything about London, Edmund!"

"You won't believe the churches, Susanna. There's hundreds of them, more than you could count," said Edmund, "their beautiful spires rising up like to touch Heaven."

Edmund had settled into a chair in the corner, draping his leg over an arm. "I'm going back as soon as I can," he said.

"My life's there, I know that now. . . . Your father did it, and now I shall too. The stage, Susanna! You should've heard the laughs, the tears those players wrung out of nowhere. It was a miracle, I tell you. . . . I've never seen anything like it."

I put down my knitting and looked at my uncle. His face was flushed pink; his hands gripped the chair.

"Promise me two things?" I asked him.

"What?"

"You must let me visit whenever I want to. I tire of this town as much as you do!"

"I promise!"

"And secondly, when you get there, and *you*, God willing, make the Swan roar with laughter or weep rivers of sorrow, please tell a certain William Shakespeare, of Stratford, that his family misses him more than anything in all this world."

Edmund got up suddenly, kissed me on the cheek, and left the room, his face lit up with joy. A few minutes later, I could hear him singing one of Father's songs in that clear, high voice of his.

> *"As shepherds feed on fields and flocks,*
> *And dullards dream 'round the clock,*
> *So country lads give up their place*
> *For roaring theaters they quicken their pace!"*

Lunatic boy! He'd better watch his step, or he'll find himself in the pit with the garlic-eating groundlings!

Stratford, March 22, 1597. Hubert has been chewing the edges of his box. What shall I do when he turns the whole thing into wood chips? Uncle Gilbert will not make another for me unless he knows why I need it. Poor Hubert. He's so little, I can't let him go now. Besides, he hasn't scared Judith half to death yet.

Stratford, March 23, 1597. Mother would not let Judith or me near the market square today. Another pillorying. Forbidden prayer books found, they say. Dull-witted rogues! Nothing I could do would convince Judith (O lily-livered one!) to take a peek, though Hamnet, the little monkey, was willing, but it was all in vain because none of us could find a way to escape from our chores. Uncle Gilbert said the man's left eye was out. What awful people they must be to hurt the helpless in the pillory. Froth and scum! These mockers of heavenly charity have no place here!

Stratford, March 24, 1597. Edmund's heading for London. He's not pretending anymore: He leaves tomorrow. Mother is most upset, but there's not much she can do about it. Father has sent word that he wants Edmund to join him for a few months. There are some openings in the London troupes as they prepare for touring the towns and villages because of plague in the city.

"I'm going, Susanna, because another river draws me," said Edmund, "the silver Thames that runs straight through the heart of London. I can hear the great Swan roaring with life, and it's calling my name, it is."

And that was it. Edmund hugged us all, received Grandfather's blessing, and will be gone before dawn tomorrow.

My heart aches with joy for Edmund. He has shown me what dreams can dare to do. God's bread! London sounds so much bigger than Swan Town, seems a place where people have space to breathe and follow their dreams. Our lovely backwater town makes Father proud, I know, but it's not so easy to live here all year round. No wonder he lives in London so much of the year. There the great stages make room for the mightiest quills.

Stratford, March 25, 1597. This year the flowers bloomed early. Judith and I helped mother make rose water today, as we do every spring. We boiled several pots, filled from the well, then mixed in the crushed petals of this year's first rose blossoms. Our fingers, clothes—the whole house—now smell of spring. Grandfather traded a pair of leather gloves for three dozen glass bottles for us to use. I have lined them up on our windowsills, where they glow in the sun.

I wonder if Edmund would like some rose water when he comes back for a visit. According to Father, the stinkards at the foot of the stage are enough to offend the strongest nose with their fumes of penny ale, so Edmund probably could use some rose water to keep him and his costumes fresh smelling.

Stratford, March 27, 1597. The house is quiet without Edmund. Too quiet. His kind, foolish ways filled our house like sunlight. Yet he was always serious about seeking a place among the London players. It is his very life, I know. Mother's face went stiff as a stone when she heard me talking to Judith about how much I would like to go to London.

Boils and plagues!

Later in the day, while I was helping Mother pull last season's stalks and weeds from our orchard, the subject came up again, this time more easily. Mother always shows her kindest side while gardening.

"Don't you go talking about leaving for London," she said. "I've heard what that city can do to a girl, I have."

"But Edmund says the theater's a magical place, and Father's genius takes wing in those playhouses, so they can't be all that bad," I said, pulling up a great clump of last year's mint and rosemary.

"Susanna, there's naught but drunkards and drabs around those theaters, and your father puts up with them as best he can. It's no place for a young girl bred in the country, I can tell you that."

"If it's so terrible, why do you put up with Father living there most of the year?" Mother paused for a moment before answering, the half smile on her face telling me she was not displeased. In the silence, I noticed the air was filled with spring smells of warm hay and early blossoms. A dove cooed in the nook of Father's attic directly behind us. Such a garden was not made for bickering. Mother knew this better than I, in truth.

"You know the carnations? The ones that flower every summer? Do you remember the legend of how they got to this island?"

"Something about a soldier—that's what Grandfather told me."

"Right," said Mother, leaning back on her strong haunches, a clump of weeds in her hand. "Their seeds were brought here by a Roman soldier, in the mud on his boots, centuries ago, and now they brighten every decent orchard in all of England. Do you see? Your father's plays are like that. They are mixed up with all sorts of low things, but they'll flower for ages and ages. And that's why I put up with his work, what little I understand of it. But that doesn't mean you need to romp in the muck to enjoy the flowers that spring from your father's pen."

Well, for all the flap-eared villains in Shoreditch, I didn't see that at all. If one has to get a little muddy to enjoy life in the theaters, well, that's all right with me. But I could hardly say that to my mother, not after her sharing such sweet thoughts with me.

Stratford, March 28, 1597. Swan Town has lost its wings. The only thing that moves around here is the river.

Stratford, March 30, 1597. This afternoon Judith and I were walking along the river when rain clouds suddenly blocked out the sun. Great rolls of thunder boomed over the meadows and across the woods and fields of Swan Town. Dunghill luck! What were we to do?

We ran as fast as we could, but before we could even get to Henley Street, the rain came down, slashing at our faces with howling winds. Holding our cloaks over our heads, we stood a moment under the eave of a house on High Street; then Mrs. Ellen Smythe opened her door across the street, and beckoned us in. Thank goodness! Mrs. Smythe is a widow who has lived alone for years, and is an acquaintance of Mother's. Seeing her smiling welcome, Judith and I ran with all our might to her open door and the promise of getting out of the rain.

"You must come out of this storm," said Mrs. Smythe, "or you will catch the cough, and there's no tellin' where that can lead." Sitting by her roaring fire, Judith and I were soon dry and very comfortable. Mrs. Smythe entertained us by telling the story about how she had met our mother many years ago at the market, while talking among the turnips and peas. She then told us about how her neighbor, Nicholas Clavering, was trying to get her to sell her back orchard to him at a cheap price. He told her that as a widow with no family, she didn't need so much land, and he could put it to better use. This neighbor, said Mrs. Smythe, also dabbled in poisonous herbs, and she feared for her garden and chickens, because he was angry that she wouldn't sell, and seemed a spiteful sort. Baseborn cur! Why should he bother a lonely woman so?

"If I ever have to sell that orchard, I'll lose much of my means of living. But all's in God's hands, my young ones, as your mother knows right well," said Mrs. Smythe, stirring her herb tea.

Once we had arrived home after the storm, Mother was saddened to hear of Mrs. Smythe's troubles with her neighbor. "When a woman isolates herself, as Ellen has done," said Mother, "she invites all sorts of rumors and difficulties. We must pray for her."

Stratford, April 4, 1597. I have killed a dozen more fleas this morning than Judith. Queen of shreds and patches! Spring is the time that all such bothersome creatures awaken. Flies hatch, fleas spring, moles burrow, bees . . . well, their buzzing is the spur that brings flowers to life, so I shouldn't complain.

And what a garden Swan Town can be! Buttercups, carnations, cowslips, daffodils, daisies, eglantines, harebells, violets, marigolds, lady's-smocks, lilies, and of course the rose. Our orchard alone boasts a dozen different roses, all of them beautiful and richly scented.

Stratford, April 7, 1597. In the early afternoon, when we finished our housework, Judith and I walked over to the market to see Grandfather and the uncles sell their goods. It was a beautiful day! The sun warmed the countless tools, saddles, gloves, baskets, copper pots, and whatnot for sale and barter that lay on the dozens of tables set up around the market. The smell of all the different spices brought from London was enchanting. Judith and I bought some honeycomb and shared it with Hamnet, who was standing alongside Grandfather's table, his face beaming with pride that he could help at market now. He's not the little tear bucket he used to be just a few years ago.

Stratford, April 12, 1597. Tasks take up most of my day now. And with little adventure to write about, my quill grows dusty and dull.

Stratford, April 30, 1597. Sprites and fires! What a chance has come my way today! Judith was walking home from market with Mother, and what did she see? A traveling band of players! Their creaky carts were making their way down Chapel Lane, toward Cutter's Field by the river. Judith and I have hatched a secret plan (it's a good thing Hamnet works most of the day in Grandfather's shop, for he could never keep this to himself). With luck, we shall do more than watch these ragged players. More anon.

Stratford, May 1, 1597. Judith and I have discovered that the players are part of the troupe that plays at the Rose, a theater on the Bankside of the Thames. Because of the plague scare in London, they are playing in country towns for several weeks, as does Father's troupe. Judith and I have decided to disguise ourselves as boy actors and have some fun before they leave town. All those stories Father has told us about his company of players have drawn me like a bee to nectar. I have always wanted to see what it's like to act upon a stage (I've had more than enough acting practice here at home). We need to find a way to mingle with the players and see just how the magic of the theater comes alive. To work, my brain.

Stratford, May 2, 1597. Earlier this evening Judith and I told Mother we were going to visit some friends. It wasn't exactly a lie—first we stopped at Griffin Tallow's house, where we put on some doublets and leather jerkins that belong to Griffin and his brothers. Griffin has been a friend of ours ever since we prayed for him several years ago when he came down with fever. We gave him a baby rabbit for a pet when he recovered, our prayers answered. He's a good sort, always reliable. He's been to London I don't know how many times. His father owns the Bear Tavern and has even studied at a university. His parents are secret believers in the old faith too, and friends with our parents, so I know we can trust him with anything.

We hid our hair under hats. From mine flowed a white feather almost a foot long, stuck in a silken band. With Griffin's whispered "Godspeed, goodly players!" we ran to Cutter's Field to watch and, although it seemed a crazy idea, maybe even to act.

The players were gathered around the back of the barn where they had drawn their carts. In front, men shouted and laughed while musicians played an interlude on the stage. Most of the audience were swilling pints of ale. By my troth! The women's bosoms swung halfway out their bodices. Judith and I stared for a few minutes, unsure of our next move. Who were these people? Surely not the same folk we see at market every day?

"It's now or never," I said.

"God's lid! Then now!" replied Judith in a shaky voice. Judith always was a little box of shivers when it came to adventures. But she tries, and that's why I love her so!

Walking to the back of the barn, we saw about a dozen players in various stages of getting ready for their show. Some were going over their lines, while others were arguing over what looked like a playbill. Three or four were still putting on their costumes, great silken robes that glowed in the light of a nearby fire that crackled angrily.

"And who might you be?" asked a voice from the darkness behind us. I spun around.

"Pardon us, sir," I said with a bow, slightly startled, "but we are two local boys looking for some work with your troupe."

Dressed in gold-cuffed black velvet, the man who emerged from the shadows was slightly taller than me. His belly looked like he had a large pillow stuffed just above his belt buckle. His whiskers were closely clipped into a beard that followed the lines of his jaw and shovel-shaped chin, and his jerkin was delicately cut, with a ruff of fine embroidery around his neck.

"Your names?"

"Richard Starling," I said.

"William Bendshaft," said Judith, with a slight smile.

Bendshaft? Shreds and patches! She was playing it close, all right.

"And your name, sir?"

"I am Bartholomew Junger, the leader of the Admiral's Men."

"Lord Howard?"

"Of course," he said, and then added, "Can you sing?"

"I can, sir," I answered. "I used to carol in church last season, and my voice is yet to break."

"Well, we are busy as you can see . . . but we can always use a boy who can sing," he said as he walked past the fire and the rest of the troupe. "Come with me, Richard, and . . ."

"William," said Judith.

"Yes, William, come with me and let me introduce you to our properties master, Roberto. He can listen to you sing, and at least see if you are any good at working. We have lots of costumes that could use cleaning, heaps of them, high as houses. Come. This way."

Before we knew what was happening, we were being led to a half circle of covered carts to the left of the barn. Roberto soon joined us. He was a tall man whose head seemed as thin as his waist. His eyes were the strangest I'd ever seen—one was blue, one was brown. The torch he held made his teeth gleam a churlish yellow.

Judith tugged at my arm. "Susanna, I don't like the looks

of this fellow. Let's go," she whispered.

"Roberto, here are the 'prentices you've been waiting for. Why don't you take these boys and see what kind of work we have for them?"

"Susanna . . ."

"Come with me—we have work enough for a village of boys," said Roberto, smiling like a jackanapes, his breath foul with ale and garlic.

Chores! That's not what we were hoping for.

"I'm not looking for common work," I said, "and neither is she. We can find enough of that in town."

"She?" said Master Junger.

"I mean he," I said quickly.

"She meant he," added Judith unhelpfully.

"*She?*" said Roberto.

"Just what do we have here?" asked Master Junger as he plucked off first my hat, then Judith's. Our long wavy hair fell out, betraying us.

"Girls?"

"Spies!" yelled Master Junger. "Who hired you? We know how to deal with spies, stealers of scripts, do we not, Roberto?"

Roberto smiled with all the charm of a rotten piece of fruit.

Now the players in back of the barn started to notice us. Several of them walked over, clearly amused at the discovery. I heard one say that finally he could now look forward to wearing some clean costumes.

Roberto grabbed Judith's arm and she screamed.

"Let go of her, you beetle-headed dolt!" I yelled.

"Come with us, script stealers," said Master Junger, grabbing my own arm and trying to lead me off in the same direction that Roberto was dragging Judith.

We were both screaming now, and pushing and kicking at these dunghill knaves who were dragging us toward some kind of everlasting servitude for their troupe. Some of the players laughed and hooted at us. I was repelled by their scullionlike manners. They were no better than the ruffians at one of our seediest local taverns. Was this the world my father wrote for? I couldn't believe it! How could these cheese breaths give life to his poetry? I started to feel dizzy with fear and confusion at the same time.

Do what we would, we couldn't free ourselves from the iron grasps of our captors. The darkened trees around us seemed to lean inward, hiding the fields and nearby lanes from sight. We were in the middle of Swan Town and about to be dragged into another world.

Then a voice with a strong Warwickshire accent rang out: "Roberto! Junger! Let go of those girls or I will run my steel through both of you!"

Uncle Edmund! God's mercy! It was him!

"Edmund, this is none of your affair. Leave us alone!" yelled Junger.

"Those two girls you have in your clutches happen to be my nieces! Now let go of them!"

Roberto and Master Junger stopped instantly and dropped our arms. By this time Edmund had his dagger drawn, ready for business.

"What?" asked Junger. "You can't be serious."

"You heard me," said Edmund, "I don't know how they got into your hands, but they're coming with me. Let Christian take my part; he knows it as well as I do."

Angry at having his plans thwarted, Master Junger quickly regained his composure.

"Be back here by the second show!" he growled.

After getting us out of the clutches of Master Junger and Roberto, Edmund marched us back home. All the while he ranted and raved at our foolishness. As we walked out of Cutter's Field to a well-trod path that ran parallel to the river, the air became cooler, and a low-lying fog clung to the ground, dimly lit by the half-moon overhead. It felt good to be rid of the players, and to be by the quiet river, though that didn't make Edmund's questions any easier to answer.

"What were you thinking?" he said. "Don't you know that most of the London troupes are a bunch of scurvy dogs when it comes to protecting their properties and scripts? Junger and Roberto are harmless enough, but they're not about to allow just anyone to snoop around their stage."

"Well, I guess I knew that," I stammered, "but didn't *you* join a troupe and make good? And in short order, too."

"I had your father's help—a man who knows every theater and every patron in London, the mighty Earl of Southampton among them. I arrived just in the knick of time, for there was an opening with this company just as they were about to leave for the countryside. You both were very, very lucky tonight. If I hadn't come along, you might have had a tough time convincing those fellows you were just in it for a laugh. Such foolishness! What's gotten into you?"

What's gotten into us? I'd like to know what's gotten into Edmund. A month with a London troupe, and he becomes Sir Oracle. I pray he's not changed for the worse. He couldn't just forget how much I longed to see the world Father and now he have made their own. Could he?

"I just thought it might be interesting to see how you and Father earn a living, that's all. . . . We didn't plan to join them," I said.

"I should hope not," answered Edmund. "All my hopes about playing on the stage . . . well, Susanna, they've been more than answered, but it's not the perfect place I dreamed about. Your father makes his living in a hard world, and the sooner you learn that, the better off you'll be."

"I quite understand my station," I added archly, "and wouldn't dream of pushing my way into your hardheaded world of stage freaks and fools."

For a minute, I thought I had gone too far. But I hated being talked to as if I were someone too delicate or too dim to comprehend the world that was my father's life. While I didn't want to seem ungrateful to Edmund for his help tonight, Judith and I aren't total beef wits. We would have thought of something!

"Don't be cross with us, Edmund—we just got carried away with an idea, one that we won't ever try again. We promise," said Judith.

"We promise," I said softly, more with my lips than my heart.

To our relief, Edmund seemed to vanquish any signs of anger. Perhaps he hadn't changed very much, after all. By Jupiter! What a delight it was to see that he was more friend than uncle when we got into trouble.

"I certainly hope not. I have to go back and try to work with those people, I do. We return to London in a few days, for the reports of plague seem to have been exaggerated. So I guess this is good-bye, for a few months at least. In the meantime, I hope you find other things to do with your time than bothering a traveling troupe, especially when I'm a part of it," he added with a smile.

As we walked over Clopton Bridge and back into town, I could hear an owl hooting in one of the willows overhanging the river. Its voice seemed to rise out of the moonlit darkness to mock Judith and me as we came at last to Henley Street and saw Grandfather's house in the distance.

After warning us again to swear off players forever, and then explaining to Mother what had happened (oh the work we're going to have to do to live this down!), Edmund gave us each a warm hug. Then he strode back to his troupe to light up their horse-drawn stage with roars of laughter and cries of calamity before they returned to London.

Mother took the news better than I thought. "Your father's love of the theater inspired him to similar antics," she said, pouring us some hot herb tea spiced with marigold blossoms. "But he was a young man, not a country lass. You two will do well to remember that. Now drink these Marybuds, and give up these foolish ways—they will come to no good, I tell you. You've housework enough here to keep you busy."

I slept restlessly that night, even after Mother's marigold tea. My mind kept drifting down all the country lanes that wandering players travel. Switches and sticks! Those players can be as cold as the stars above, especially when they're protecting their scripts. Yet despite their scurvy manners, their robes and richly embroidered costumes still hint of the magic they can bring to the stage. Somehow I have a feeling we are not done with them yet.

Stratford, May 4, 1597. Griffin Tallow laughed like a tipsy rover when we told him of our misadventures.

Hamnet hasn't been much help either. After Judith told him about our encounter with Edmund's troupe, he has been scampering around with a wooden sword, pretending that he is Master Junger or Roberto, and asking us in his best fiendish voice if we know what happens to script stealers and pinchers of properties.

Stratford, May 5, 1597. A friend of Mother's stopped by today, on his way to London. Mother gave him a brief letter to deliver to Father at the theater. I gave him my best quill pen to give to Uncle Edmund, a left-handed scribbler like myself. It's the least I can do after all his help. The one I chose for Edmund was very long, and touched with delicate streaks of gray, like a sky at sunset.

Stratford, May 6, 1597. This morning I could tell that something was bothering Grandfather. He told Judith and me not to stir from the house today. As Grandfather sat brooding by the kitchen fire, I rolled my eyes in the direction of the back of the house and walked out. Judith met me behind a mulberry tree Father had planted the day she was born.

"Sister, we can't stay here and cower like church mice," I told her. "Something's afoot in town today, and I want to see it with my own eyes."

"You'll get us into trouble, Susanna," said Judith like the snail-hearted one she often is.

"I for one don't want to die in the shadows like some spinster who won't taste anything more thrilling than her lukewarm cider. Come on!"

Judith knew enough not to argue. We had been through this kind of tussle before, and I was used to having my way. Grandfather was soon busy in the shop, and Mother was safely in the kitchen. We quietly sneaked away.

Once on our way down Chapel Street, we could see a crowd gathering around the Guild Chapel. A few shouts, and one or two hats tossed into the air, made it seem as if some kind of holiday were under way. Judith and I walked closer, sensing that something was wrong even amid all the smiles and festive faces.

Sir Colin Hill and his rat-faced men were standing in front of the chapel doors. They held axes and monstrously sized maces in their hands, as if they had come to do battle with some gigantic tree that had dared to grow where they wouldn't allow it. Two or three of the men also carried paint pots and brushes.

"Let's get on with it now, shall we? I hereby reclaim this chapel from all popish pretenders and cleanse it of all images and structures contrary to the true faith of this land. Stand away. All who heed shall not be harmed!" Sir Colin declared.

He led his men into the chapel, and more than a dozen people followed, their eyes bright with mischief and delight at what was about to happen. Judith and I were the last to enter, and when we did, Sir Colin and his men were already hard at it.

Toad-spotted infidels! They were attacking the chapel!

Sir Colin's minions were painting plaster over the decorated walls. Holy images from the Gospels, gorgeous scenes of saints sketched centuries ago, all were targets. Sir Colin himself led several men to the rood loft, where the blessed body of our Lord clung high to a golden cross. They ripped the entire loft from its base and carried it out to a waiting horse cart. Then the maces swung into action, splintering the altar rail into scrap wood.

Finally, as if saving the last blow for the most important symbol, they smashed the marble altar into dozens of pieces and tossed them on the waiting cart outside. Soon they replaced it with a simple table more in keeping, I gather, with the changes dictated by their own brutish ideas of religion. Damned villains!

Judith followed me out and we made our way home. The brick-fronted houses of Swan Town stared impassively at us as if nothing unusual had happened this morning. Why, for some it was a festival! Marble-hearted tyrants!

"How could these men destroy such beauty in the name of God?" I asked. "What has God to do with such hateful spite? Father always taught us that beauty was one of the Creator's handiworks, that whatever glows with its special fineness comes from on high, from the God of all. And now they have destroyed a chapel crafted by men long gone, generations of beauty blasted in a single morning. It's not right, I tell you!"

Judith held my hand. I felt as if a part of me had just been torn out and thrown away. Perhaps there is no way to win against such powers other than Father's way of acting high upon a stage, with one's own heart hidden from the rabble and the powers of the crown. But how could that be my way? I felt doubly boxed in now, both by Her Majesty's crude ministers, banishing a faith rooted in this land, and by the dreadfully boring lives that others ordain for girls, before we're even born or old enough to show what talents we have. Newts and blindworms, but I must find my way somehow!

Stratford, May 8, 1597. I spent the day with Mother and Judith working in the back garden. We cut more than a dozen young herbs to hang over the kitchen fireplace. The warm scent of drying mint brought ease to my mind.

Yet dark thoughts still haunt me about what our elders have done to Swan Town. Whenever I have to walk by the chapel now, my neck stiffens and I want to cry out to Heaven for the harm done by Sir Colin and his ruthless men. I am going to ask Grandfather if he knows a different way to the market, a way to avoid altogether the chapel they have defaced and betrayed.

Stratford, May 9, 1597. There's disturbing talk about some recent strange events, of which I had heard little until tonight. Mother told us the story as we made dinner. It concerns witchcraft, supposedly practiced in Stratford by Ellen Smythe, the kind but lonely widow who helped Judith and me only a few weeks ago. Such foolishness! Mrs. Smythe would never hurt anyone, as Judith and I know firsthand.

The case is to be tried in the local court any day now. According to Mother, Mrs. Smythe spoke sharply to a ten-year-old girl named Susan Webster after the little girl wandered repeatedly into Mrs. Smythe's herb garden.

Immediately after returning home, Susan became ill, crying continually, "Leave me alone, witch, oh leave me alone!" She died that night. Later, the distraught mother found seven of her chickens dead without a wound on them. Mrs. Webster has taken the case to the council, which has summoned Mrs. Smythe to a hearing. Until then she must remain in her house except for the hour between eleven and noon.

According to our high and mighty town council, we have witches in Stratford. Sots! I believe none of them.

Stratford, May 10, 1597. Mrs. Smythe's case comes before the court in three days. You would have thought a town festival was about to take place when the council announced the date. Little boys and beastly mannered young men hooted, fought, and smiled as if on holiday. She's as good as convicted!

There is something about this case that smells of something other than witchcraft, but I don't know what it is. Poor Mrs. Smythe! The town council could sentence her to ducking, branding, pressing under stones, or even worse.

Stratford, May 11, 1597. Judith and I were talking about the afternoon we spent with Mrs. Smythe, and we remembered the problems she was having with her neighbor. Since we know the idea of witchcraft is so preposterous, we can't help but wonder if somehow that has something to do with these charges. Since she wouldn't sell her land to Mr. Clavering willingly, getting her in trouble with the council would be a way for him to get his hands on her property. We shared Mrs. Smythe's story with Grandfather, and he seemed particularly interested in the part about Nicholas Clavering's poisonous herbs.

Grandfather said, "There are things here that add up to nothing more than the devils we know, rather than the witches we sometimes imagine. I'll look into it, girls, fear not."

Stratford, May 12, 1597. Mrs. Smythe's case is scheduled for tomorrow. Grandfather visited some neighbors of hers and then spent the better part of the day talking with various folk in and around Swan Town. He returned shortly before dinner, very upset at the news he had heard.

"The council will be damned in their own minds if they don't find a witch in this town, I know it, but there's not a shred of evidence that convinces me that Mrs. Smythe is guilty," he said, sitting down at the table. "And talking to some of Clavering's other neighbors, what did I find? Tales of poisoned livestock, going back of ten years or more. The lust for land often goes by the path of poison. I've seen it more times than I care to admit."

"What are we to do then?" Mother asked. "I can't bear to think of that poor woman going up against the town council all by herself. You must help her, John. You had great influence in this town years ago. Surely you can do something."

"Tomorrow I'll go to the councilmen and speak my piece. If I need to get sworn statements, well, I'll get them is all."

Stratford, May 13, 1597. Today, the gray-bearded idiots of Swan Town pronounced sentence on Mrs. Smythe. Grandfather left early to try to convince the council to consider hearing the testimony of several neighbors against Clavering in the decision, but he was rudely turned away by the councilmen. He returned to our house before noon, his face flushed with anger at the foolishness of these men. Mother sat by the fire and quietly prayed. Those brutes! How could they refuse to listen to a man such as Grandfather? Were they so desperate to find a witch that any woman would do?

Judith and I had already agreed that we would quietly slip out of the house in order to witness the judgment and, if necessary, witness Mrs. Smythe's punishment. All the while, we would pray for her soul's deliverance.

As soon as we rounded the corner of High Street, we saw a huge crowd gathered at either end of Clopton Bridge.

"They're going to duck her!" cried Judith. "That's the only reason why they'd be at the bridge."

"My God, you're right!" I panted, out of breath as we both stopped running and moved into the jeering crowd.

We had missed the sentencing. The town bailiff, with his fur collar and staff, stood high on the bridge's center stone, his face pink, and his eyes shining in the breeze. Around him stood the councilmen of the town, with Sir Colin Hill looking on at the grim proceedings. I noticed Mrs. Webster standing with a member of the town council. Her face was as pale as whey. The wind lightly ruffled the surface of the river, which glided slowly by us all.

Mrs. Smythe herself stood in the center of the bridge.

She was surrounded by armed men, their maces and weapons mutely threatening anyone who dared break into the circle that held Mrs. Smythe as tightly as any prison. With a huge murmur, the crowd turned to watch several men carry the ducking stool to the center of the bridge. I grasped Judith's hand, wanting with all my might to run up on the bridge, poke Sir Colin in the eye, and throw the horrid device into the Avon.

"Proceed!" yelled the bailiff. "And let all citizens of Stratford see what foul pollutions come from consorting with the devil. May the waters of our ancient river wash this woman clean, and may the example of her suffering per-suade all souls to follow the path of righteousness today and forevermore! To the glory of our most high God and Her Majesty, Queen Elizabeth!"

"No! You can't . . . please, I beg you . . . I am innocent of these charges, I am!" implored Mrs. Smythe, whose cries went to my heart as keenly as sharpened arrows. None of the officials on the bridge so much as blinked.

"Tie and gag her," ordered Sir Colin.

For a moment, I thought I would fall right into the flowing river. The earth seemed to become as thin as any parchment. Why would these good people of Swan Town go along with such horrors? The world seemed to have gone mad.

With an uncanny swiftness, the ducking stool was brought forth. In one sweeping movement Mrs. Smythe was pushed into the chair—its back was fixed with an overhead arrangement of ghastly wheels and ropes—and with some struggle tied down. They lifted her over the side of the bridge as Sir Colin muttered some words, and then the men holding the lines let their ends of the rope go.

The stool, with Mrs. Smythe strapped to it, splashed into the water.

Then she was under. The crowd let out a collective gasp, as if it felt the cold water sting their limbs instead of Mrs. Smythe's. A group of children and two or three dogs scrambled to the banks of the river to see more closely. After a certain count, the men yanked on the ropes, and Mrs. Smythe and the ducking stool emerged, dripping and streaming water.

Judith and I slowly moved away from the bridge. I looked once again at Mrs. Smythe's shrunken figure, lashed to the stool. It was hard to be sure if she was still breathing. She seemed to me at that moment the very portrait of sorrow.

Condemned to such humiliation and pain, and for what? To satisfy the dark imaginings of townsfolk afraid of their own shadows? To restore Swan Town to the true faith?

"Duck her again! The devil in such women is particularly strong," said Sir Colin.

Judith tugged my sleeve. "I'm going," she said. "I can't bear to see her go in again." For once my sister was right. With pale faces and trembling knees, we ran back to Henley Street. Before we were twenty paces from the bridge, however, I heard the terrible whirr of the ropes falling, falling, and the splash of Mrs. Smythe's plunge into the cold waters of the river. Such sounds will haunt me for the rest of my days, almost as much as the murmurs of approval I heard coming from the crowds gathered for her ducking.

Stratford, May 14, 1597. Mrs. Smythe died today. The ducking imposed by the town fathers brought on ague, of which she died early this morning, shaking in a fit of fever and delirium. After Grandfather told us the news, I quickly excused myself and left. Judith started to follow, but I waved her off. After a few minutes of walking, I found myself running down our street, and then on to the wide meadows by the river. I had to be alone. This horrible act of cruelty struck my heart like a lance.

God have mercy on Mrs. Smythe. God have mercy on me for the thoughts that come into my brain after such injustice. How can the people of Swan Town be so cruel? Scurvy, railing tyrants!

As I walked across the meadow, thousands of lady's-smocks and buttercups formed a delicate carpet all around me.

My tears turned them into a blur of color in a patchwork of sunlight and shade. Sitting under an elm tree, I tried to gather my thoughts about what was happening in this crazy town of fear and now such knavish violence.

Two large hawks circled overhead. A cool breeze blew, sending shivers through the grass and the wildflowers that swayed back and forth. Perhaps the birds scented something on the wind, the fallen body of a deer or fox.

I stared south, at Trinity's tower and the narrow rooftops of our little town. The river ran past Clopton Bridge, the scene of Mrs. Smythe's punishment, now bearing no trace of that awful crime. The tears kept coming. Why had the council not believed Grandfather, not even listened to him? The shadows of the hawks circling over the field swept back and forth.

My mind was sensible of little more than the hurt I felt deep inside of me. What was this world we lived in? A prison? How could that be, with such meadows as this?

Suddenly I felt the sun on my dress. The shade under the elm had vanished. Now the entire meadow caught the morning sun, its flowers glowing like yellow fire riding the high grass. This lovely meadow became in my mind's eye an image of the world. I saw it filled with beautiful flowers of every type, but with nettles and crowflowers too. I also saw it haunted by high-flying evil ones, like the hawks above me, who may cast long shadows but are unable to uproot the wildflowers that bloom year after year, sown by the hand of God.

Something lifted from my heart. I now saw—almost all at once—what I had to do. I must join my family in their practice of the old faith. Only divine charity can overcome such darkness and ill will. As I walked back to our house, I felt a peace in my soul. With weapons as old as the Apostles, I would fight the madness that had taken over this land. But first I had to get my Grandfather's permission.

Stratford, May 15, 1597. I spent much of this morning waiting for an opportunity to ask Grandfather the question that has finally come to full bloom in my heart. Shortly before noon, while doing needlework on a pair of kid gloves, I saw my opportunity as he took a break from his own stitching work. Now was the time.

"Grandfather, I have a question, if you please."

"Yes, my dear, what is it?"

"I'd like to stop going to the established church," I said. I was secretly pleased I didn't mangle the words but said them clearly and with confidence. Softly, Grandfather asked why. Watching how the old faith had been so savagely persecuted, I now knew how precious it was to me, I told him, more precious than any worldly treasure or comfort. The day was sunny, and warm waves of light streamed through the open windows. But with his face going paler by the second, Grandfather seemed a ghost.

"Child, come walk with me, for this kind of question needs more airing than this room can give, I can tell you that."

We went down to Holy Trinity and strolled up and down the avenue, amid the lime trees bending gently in the breeze off the river. Gradually we made our way to our family's graves. There Grandfather reminded me that the times, though better than in generations past, were still dangerous.

"Right now you dream of fighting for your right to believe as you will, and that's as it should be. But days will come when such a path may cost more than perhaps you can bear, more than you can imagine. Sometimes troubles must be borne. Sometimes they must be resisted. Are you ready to learn the difference? And do what the day demands?"

"I am, I promise," I said solemnly.

"And will you remember in your soul that amid the weeds and tares of this island, good souls follow all kinds of faiths, not just ours? God's spirit blows where it will. Never forget that as long as you live."

"I'll remember. I promise I will."

"You are your father's child," he said with a chuckle, "and so learn faster than most, praise God. You're much like these swans that have been keeping our river company since long before I was a boy."

"What do you mean?"

Grandfather stroked his beard and smiled at me.

"Our swans are graceful and strong and, perhaps most of all, too curious for their own good. They think they own the river that runs through our town, and by God, they do. They are also great jesters and have been known to smirk at the fools crossing Clopton Bridge many a day. And you, my dear girl, are all of these things, whether you know it or not."

I blushed a little at Grandfather's compliment (at least I think it was a compliment) but was determined to push on with my request.

"So I may worship with you?"

"You'll go with us, to be sure, Susanna, but you must be as silent as these mossy stones if you don't want to make martyrs of half the town—and of all your family," he said in that low, warm voice of his. "And remember, unlike a swan, you can't just fly away and leave your troubles behind. Do you understand me, girl?"

"I do, Grandfather, God's faith, I do," was all I could say. All that needed to be said. And that's how I became a "traitor" to the crown. As simple as breathing.

Stratford, May 16, 1597. Kites and buzzards! Judith was practically in tears over my decision to leave the established church and attend secret masses. She told me a woman in the Johnson house had just yesterday delivered a baby with the great flapping ears of a dog and a long, snoutlike nose.

"Such signs hold nothing good, I know," she said, nervously shelling hazelnuts by the fireplace.

"You acorn!" I told her. "Doesn't growing up mean you get to decide yourself how to live, how to believe? Pish! I don't know about you, but the more days I see, the more I don't like someone else making up my own mind for me!" Though I do love Judith, she simply must grow up. After all, fitting in isn't everything, and the only dog-eared men in Swan Town are the churls atop our pulpits!

Stratford, May 17, 1597. Today, Hamnet and I put Hubert inside Judith's left slipper, early in the morning, to cheer her up after our fight over her fears yesterday. Oh the screams! I marvel at how my sister can take fright at her own shadow, or the shadow of a silly mouse. Though some days I think they are one and the same! Afterward I let Hubert go. He had earned his freedom.

Mother showed me one of Grandfather's old prayer books this evening. It was a pocket-size missal printed in 1557.

"We must never speak of such a book to any outside this house, on your honor and the love you bear for your family. Such books are forbidden by Her Majesty's ministers, and they are reaching out to all parts of this land to destroy all reminders of the old faith."

As Mother carefully turned the pages, one in particular caught my eye, and I motioned for her to pause a moment. On it was the paternoster, the great prayer taught us by God himself, by his only Son. All around the magnificent *P* of "Pater" were garlanded flowers that looked like wild hyacinths. Azure-blue petals curled out of green stems, while a brightly painted bird, no more than a house sparrow in size and shape, lifted its beak toward the heavens beyond the page's gilded margins, and sang its heart out.

Stratford, May 18, 1597. Hamnet skinned three kid goats today with as high a degree of skill as I've ever seen. He's attentive and has a quicker knife than his father, or at least that's what Grandfather says. Though Hamnet says he doesn't like the greasy feeling of the skins on his hands, Uncle Gilbert says he'll get used to it. I wonder. Hamnet shows only a passing interest in stage plays, but he's clever enough, no doubt. The questions that he asks! His little brain never stops, I swear. For instance, this morning he asked us: If the queen sneezes, and her soul flees her body, is the kingdom momentarily without a monarch?

Stratford, May 20, 1597. Grandfather took me to hear mass at a hidden chapel on a farm some three miles from town. There were about ten others there with us, each grateful for this opportunity of grace and prayer. The smell of the beeswax candles made me sleepy but very content. Sir Colin Hill's marble heart seemed a world away.

Stratford, May 22, 1597. While Judith and I were washing clothes and linens in the kitchen before hanging them out to dry in the fragrant air of our back orchard, Mother and Hamnet went to the market to buy some spices. We had two large pots of water boiling as we twisted and soaked and soaked and twisted the steaming garments clean. The house was quiet except for some finches outside the window, fluttering and chirping, looking for cast-off bits of stale bread.

When we finished, I carried one of the pots of still-warm water to the door to splash over the stones in front of our house.

"Get the door for me, Judith, will you?"

When she opened the door, I heaved up the first heavy pot (I may be on the thin side, but my arms are strong enough), and when I looked up, I was staring into Father's face! Judith screamed in delight, and I promptly dropped the pot to the ground. The water leaped into the air, soaking my dress and covering me and Father with white frothy soap suds.

"My dear, that white beard doesn't become you in the least," he said, grinning.

As soap bubbles floated into the air, I felt for my face, and sure enough, there was a long beard of suds across my face and down my neck. But what did I care what I looked like? Both Judith and I rushed to give Father a great big hug and kiss. To see him after so many months filled our hearts to bursting. His face flushed with pleasure as he blessed us and wiped his boots dry after running into my soapy welcome.

"Come, tell me everything I've missed while away—silly or serious, I want to hear it," he said. "How much you've both grown, and so pretty. I am a rich man indeed."

We were soon sitting at the table by the kitchen fireplace, laughing and sharing tales of the time we had spent apart. Father told us of how a man had fallen asleep at one of his plays, and how one of the players had stolen his breeches. When the play ended, the man stood up, and only after hearing howls of laughter did he realize his bare bottom was in view of the entire playhouse. He fled amid gales of laughter and a storm of hazelnut shells.

The jokes Father tells always send me and Judith into fits of laughter. Using one of his quill pens, he drew faces on some walnut shells, props for a story about twins in love with the same woman. The voices he can conjure up! You'd think a whole troupe of players was in our kitchen. All Father needs is the palm of his hand and a few items from the shelf. Trolls alive! He has stage enough!

We even played word-pudding, a game he taught us when we were very young. The goal is to pile up words as if they were pudding, and whoever can think up the most words without hesitating—that's the hard part—wins the game. Naturally, Father is a master of such battles, but I love trying to tangle with his wit, even if I rarely succeed in such efforts.

"A knave," said father.

"A foul-mouthed knave," I answered.

"A foul-mouthed, gor-bellied knave," he countered.

"A foul-mouthed, gor-bellied, worsted-stocking knave."

"A foul-mouthed, gor-bellied, worsted-stocking, calumnious knave."

"A foul-mouthed, gor-bellied, worsted-stocking, calumnious, whoreson, beetle-headed knave," I volleyed.

"A foul-mouthed, gor-bellied, worsted-stocking, calumnious, whoreson, beetle-headed, garlic-fuming knave," Father effortlessly fired back.

Trying with all my might to avoid looking at Judith, who was laughing with delight at Father's apparent victory, I took a deep breath and racked my brains for another sally.

"A foul-mouthed, gor-bellied, worsted-stocking, calumnious, whoreson, beetle-headed, garlic-fuming . . . doting knave!"

"A foul-mouthed, gor-bellied, worsted-stocking, calumnious, whoreson, beetle-headed, garlic-fuming, doting, three-suited, hundred-pound, fantastical knave!"

"My wit is out, Father, I admit it!"

"Susanna," he said, "your wit is just beginning, I daresay. There's no telling what that fertile brain of yours is capable of brewing up."

Now it was my turn to flush. Father's praise was sweeter than honey, and it thrilled me to my toes.

When Mother finally arrived home, she and Father hugged for the longest time. When they finally parted, he said, "I could have the whole world at my fingertips, Anne, but it wouldn't keep me from missing you."

"You have a whole city of theaters," Mother said, laughing, "and you still miss me? Now that's a pretty saying for my heart, it is."

I saw Father take some papers from his satchel and put them carefully into Mother's hands. More love poems, I suspect. Mother folded them into her the bosom of her dress.

That's the last we'll ever hear of them, I'm sure. Some things we can share with only a single soul.

Father lifted Hamnet up over his head, spinning round with joy to see him. Hamnet then brandished his wooden sword and showed Father some fencing moves he had learned from Grandfather.

Later that evening we dined royally: stewed venison, a herring pie, and a wonderful dish of buttered eggs with anchovies. Judith pleased everyone with her bacon tart. The delicious smell wafted through the house, a fine feast for the return of our father.

After dinner I told him of my decision to practice the old faith. He seemed pleased. He told me that the times dictated especial care and extreme caution. "Remember to judge the tree by its fruit, and not its pretty blossoms," he told me before bed, "and never esteem any man by the faith he professes, but by the deeds he puts his hand to."

Stratford, May 23, 1597. Hamnet came running into the shop at noon all out of breath to tell us that the body of a dog was floating down the Avon. Scores of people were watching as the strange sight drifted by. Mother forbade him to go near the animal.

Stratford, May 24, 1597. Plague has come to our town, though, thanks be to God, not nearly as bad as past years. And of course it's often much worse in London, so we are glad Father is here with us. Grandmother says that she thinks the year of Father's birth was the worst, taking away nearly two hundred souls from Swan Town in one season.

It's an awful way to die, I hear. Mother says your body is racked with fevers, chills colder than the heart of winter, and your groin and armpits become swelling sores that burst in blood and pus. Blood comes up with your hacking cough until your eyes roll back in death. By'r Lakin! May the Lord deliver us!

Stratford, May 25, 1597. Hyssop. *Hyssopus officinalis*. A bitter but useful herb, especially in time of plague. Mother says it heals body and soul. Cleanse me, O Lord, and I shall be whiter than your swans.

Stratford, May 26, 1597. This afternoon Father copied out in fine flowing hand some speeches for my birthday. His *A Midsummer Night's Dream* is filled with magical creatures, enough to dazzle any audience. Hamnet prowls about the house, playing, he says, the part of Puck. Puck's a spirit of the forest who pulls chairs from under old maids and tips over buckets of milk in barns, serving the creature known as Oberon by making as much mischief as possible.

Wit snapper! My brother was born for that role.

Later on, Mother and Father took a walk after dinner. Seeing we had an opportunity, I asked Judith to join me in acting out some of Father's lines from his play *The Comedy of Errors*. He had left the pages on a table in the kitchen, so I thought he wouldn't mind us borrowing it for an hour or so.

Hamnet held a glowing lantern outside the window, projecting light as I had directed him. Judith played my master, looking for me, the servant. Both characters have twins, providing no end of mischief. Working from Father's manuscript, I changed these two characters into women—and with much justice, for the menfolk of Swan Town can be an onerous sort!

> *The Scene: At a tavern. Enter Susanna, as servant,*
> *clothed in wit, and Judith as lady of the house,*
> *dressed in a long, silken gown with a slightly*
> *mangy rabbit-fur collar. Hamnet as moonlight.*

Our stage was the hearth before the fireplace in the main room off the kitchen. I entered by the stairwell, Judith by the front door. Hamnet crouched outside the open window, his lantern at the ready. The light from the fading fire was dim and so suited our scene. Roasting hickory nuts over the grate gave the setting a warm, tavernlike atmosphere.

Judith and I entered the room at the precisely the same moment and collided with each other.

"Why, how now, Drusilla? Where runn'st thou so fast?" asked Judith in a ridiculous attempt to imitate a matron's voice.

"I am fleeing a man, and no one else," I replied breathlessly.

"What man? And how beside thyself?" asked Judith.

"Marry, my lady, beside myself, I am due to a man; one that claims me, one that haunts me, one that will have me!"

"What claim lays he to thee?"

"Marry, lady, such claim as you would lay to your horse." Here Hamnet whinnied, causing our moonlight to quiver most unnaturally. I shot him a severe look and he stopped. I wanted this scene to have at least some resemblance to proper acting.

After all, we were a theater family; our name was known in all the theaters in London. Silly coxcomb! We had a reputation to protect!

At this point the script called for a marvelously inventive description of the most odious rascal who ever sought a woman's hand. Yet as Judith began making a mishmash of many of her lines, I gently shoved her to one side.

"What man seeks my hand? Why, he's the kitchen knave, and all grease; and I know not what use to put him to, but to make a lamp of him, and run from him by his own light. If he lives till doomsday, he'll burn a week longer than the whole world. His complexion is like my shoe. His breadth is spherical, like a globe; I could find countries in him! Where Ireland? In his buttocks: I found it out by the bogs. Where France? In his forehead, armed and making war against his hair. England? In his chin, by the salt rheum that ran between France and his neck. Spain? Faith! I saw it not; but I felt it hot in his breath! The Netherlands? Oh, my lady, I did not look so low."

This last line made my face blush red with embarrassment. Judith collapsed on a chair, holding her side from laughing so hard. Hamnet had stopped laughing as soon as he figured out the joke was on him and all blunt-witted men the world over. Knot-pated rascal!

Suddenly, Father stuck his head into the room, a mischievous look on his face. We all stood stock-still, caught in the act, so to speak.

"Bravo! Not bad, Susanna, not bad at all. If you were born a male child like your brother, I could see you taking the stage by storm," he said. "However, someday I suspect you'll feel differently about boys, you and Judith. They won't remain the rude rascals you think they are today."

"I think it's wrong women aren't allowed to act," I said, somewhat angrily. Father's point about boys wasn't worth a response, utterly cracked as it was.

"They act more than you think, my dear, just not on the stage."

"It's a matter of being true to our talents, no more. To thine own self be true, as I have heard you say many a time."

Before Father could respond, Mother pushed her way into the room and declared that it was time for bed.

Hamnet fled without a word. Father seemed lost in thought as he distractedly kissed Judith and me both good-night, and we went up to our room, leaving him and Mother downstairs by the fire. Was he thinking about the justice of my reply? Probably not. I'd wager he was thinking about a new play instead.

As I drifted off to sleep, I couldn't help but wonder how I would do penning lines of my own someday. After all, didn't Father himself say that I have a fertile brain? Writing, not playing, could be my ticket out of this sleepy town that would tether me to a life as narrow as any barn. It certainly would be easier than clipping my hair and hiding my bosom (such as it is) and trying to sneak a part in some play I had no hand in. To thine own self be true? We shall see!

Stratford, May 28, 1597. Father left today for London. His business in Swan Town settled, he needs to get back to his theater fellows. I don't feel like writing any more today.

Stratford, May 29, 1597. I have been helping Grandfather set up his stock of spring ale, rolling the heavy barrels into a back corner of the cellar. Uncles Gilbert and Richard have several times urged him to open one barrel, "to test the batch," they say. But Grandfather has shown me how to watch the skies, and I know that the new moon coming in three weeks will show our ale fit for princes.

Stratford, May 30, 1597. Hamnet has been working hard in Grandfather's shop, and when the candles are burning low, he's still helping with all the orders that seem never to have an end.

Stratford, June 1, 1597. I sometimes wonder how Mother gets along without Father. She says she keeps busy enough that the time flies between his visits. If I ever marry—what strange-sounding words—I don't know if I could let my husband (listen to me!) leave for half the year at a time.

Stratford, June 4, 1597. Due to Grandmother's attempts at warding off the sickness, the whole house smells of lavender and rosemary and rue. The shop is safe from her efforts. Pish! Nothing can replace the sharp smell of tanner's work.

Stratford, June 5, 1597. Hamnet is sick with plague. This afternoon he started coughing and wheezing, rapidly becoming so weak and feverish, he had to be put to bed. Gilbert and Richard have ridden to London to get Father. Dr. Markson is with Hamnet but holds out little hope. There is blood in the spittle, he says.

Stratford, June 6, 1597. Today, shortly before noon, my brother Hamnet died.

I was allowed upstairs only for a moment after he died, though earlier, in my room, I could hear everything. His coughing. The flutter of live pigeons as they were laid to his plague sores (an old remedy and, I know now, a useless one). Then, later, the heavy pushing about of furniture as Hamnet's body was wrapped and carried out on the bed he died on. The bed was burned within the hour. Hamnet will be buried tomorrow.

The swift hand of death. How you have cheated us of such a small, smiling boy, I have the tears to tell.

Father should arrive in a few days. I know his heart will break. For all my life I have believed in a mythical Heaven, laced with endless cloud, but now, now that my brother is gone, I know the truth: Heaven is as real as death is sad.

Stratford, June 11, 1597. Father arrived late last night. Edmund simply couldn't leave, as his role in a play this week demanded his presence in London. Judith and I were asleep when Father rode in. In the middle of the night, I awoke to the sound of terrible, heart-wrenching sobs. I knew right away it was Father. I could hear Mother's voice, soothing him. I shall never forget that night as long as I live. Nor the brave face Father put on in the morning, as he led us in prayer at Hamnet's grave, his heart struck with sorrow, yet his faith still shining bright in the darkness of it all.

Griffin's family has been most kind to us. Each day this week his mother has helped Mother prepare and cook dinner. Such charity eases the hours, especially for Mother.

Stratford, June 12, 1597. Sorrow seems to come in waves, from some hidden and endless sea. This afternoon Mother in forgetfulness set a place for Hamnet at the table. She even included his favorite cup, which Grandfather had carved from an elm branch. All of us, I am afraid, made a bad show of it, as our tears flowed again. Later, while trying to fall asleep, I couldn't shake from my mind the last glimpse I was allowed of Hamnet before he was taken out and buried. His arms were folded as he lay on the bed, his hands at either elbow. His face was pale and smaller somehow. Mother's sobs echo through my head like some terrible song I will never forget.

Stratford, June 13, 1597. What would I give just to see our little Puck again? The world would not be too much.

Stratford, June 14, 1597. A week now since we buried Hamnet. Judith is doing the best she can, what with the loss of her twin. He was such a strong boy, always into everything. We thought he'd merely become tired, helping with the skins and all the work he'd do in the garden, keeping it right for Father's visits. When they came.

Father goes back to London tomorrow. While I know that his heart as a player and poet belongs to that city, I still can't bear to see him leave us. God's bodkin! It's not easy being the daughter to such a rabble pleaser as our father!

Stratford, June 15, 1597. The warm air makes the light on our river hazy. At dusk I can almost see the plague dancing across Clopton Bridge, its brow blacker than the foulest devil's.

Stratford, June 16, 1597. Last evening three swans flew by the house toward the river. With the windows open, we could hear their great white wings creaking across the darkening sky. One of the swans flew slightly ahead of the other two. Grandfather looked up at me, and said: "Like Hamnet, that one . . . ahead of us, but never far from our hearts." As Grandfather wiped his eyes, he told me about the legend of the swan.

"Swans don't usually do much more than hiss and cluck," he said, "except when they know their last hour is near. Then they send forth a song that would move the heart of man and beast. Heaven notes their sorrow, so beautiful is it, and know, my child, that Heaven heeds your own. Never doubt that, in all your life."

Dear Grandfather, I will remember, I promise. But right now all I want to do is fold my wings and sleep.

Stratford, June 17, 1597. Judith and I spent half the day walking along the river. The air had cooled, and the silent flow of the water gathered our thoughts, pulling them into one stream, our brother's death.

"It's like looking up at a cloudless sky," said Judith, when I asked her how it felt to have lost her twin.

Judith not being given to poetry, I didn't understand her right away.

"The sky usually has a cloud or two you can count on to give you a sense of distance, of being here and not there. That's what Hamnet was for me, his voice, his smile, his silly little jokes," she explained. "How they would drive me to distraction, and how I could never resist either laughing at him or throwing something at him. His voice reminded me just where I was. The sound, I think, of home. Well, now that voice is gone. The sky is empty. There's nothing now."

"Sister," I said, putting my arm around her, "we must not tempt Heaven, you see, for we have the bittersweet gift of a brother who is now there. And if *you* couldn't resist his boyish charm, do you really think the angels can?"

Judith wiped her eyes and laughed. We sat by Clopton Bridge for the rest of the afternoon, watching the currents shoot past us, swirling on the sun-flecked surface until they disappeared down the river.

Stratford, June 18, 1597. The streets outside our house are quiet, as men from the town council set the plague fires. More than ten homes lost members of their families this year. The smoke billows black and deadly, for a time even blocking out the sun.

Stratford, June 19, 1597. Although my decision to practice the old faith has helped soothe my soul, I can no longer simply watch Swan Town become a hammer for tyranny and injustice. I am going to fight it. Yes, I know what you're thinking. I am just a girl, with straw-colored hair and bony fingers. What can I do?

Well, for one thing I can write. I am going to pen a play. I am going to muster as much cleverness as is in my brain and write a play about this ridiculous kingdom that drowns innocent women, while a witch sits on the throne and her evil minions inspire fear throughout the land. Now, after Hamnet's death, I see how there are no tomorrows granted any of us with certainty. Besides, as Father has said many times, self-love is not so vile a sin as self-neglecting. Well, I'll just show how right he is!

I plan to call my play *The Celebrated History of the Parrot King*. It shall expose this island as the place of stupid parroting it has become, where too many echo only what's pleasing to those in authority, be it the minister, the mayor, the lord, or the queen herself. I shall lance the boils of stupidity that afflict this country with such fear that no one feels free to believe or speak as conscience demands. If the authorities protest, I will just point out that my play is based on nothing but ancient fables. As Aesop had speaking animals in his stories, so will mine, and therefore they can do no harm. I shall find a way to make the groundlings in the pit howl at the follies of this ill-sorted kingdom!

Judith shall know only after I have finished writing it. Father shall know only after it is performed at the theater!

Stratford, June 20, 1597. I have started my play today. Beginnings are always the hardest part, but I like it well enough. The rhymes are really just playing word-pudding with yourself. It makes me feel good to set the stupidities of our kingdom in their proper place, even if my masterpiece may never be staged. Though there's always hope!

Stratford, June 21, 1597. I worry about Judith and how different she seems after the death of Hamnet. We've all changed, I know that. I sense in myself a greater daring, a trust in something like luck, or Providence, even. This change is what has kept me going in my decision to write my play.

But Judith seems to have become more timid, if that's possible. Many a day, after her work is done, I see her sitting by the fireplace, staring at nothing in particular, or just walking alone by the river, her eyes red and puffy from crying, roaming the same paths that she and Hamnet used to run down with such fun. Perhaps this is one more reason to write my *Parrot King*. Judith is a girl who needs adventure. Sprites and fires! My play might just be the thing that will help her live her life outside the shadow of Hamnet's death. I must share it with her.

Stratford, June 22, 1597. Last night I dreamed Hamnet was in my room, sitting on the chair by my desk. He looked just as I remember him, except his legs disappeared into the shadowy light that pooled around the floor. He watched me for a minute or so, then, smiling slightly, put his finger to his lips and vanished.

I awoke to hear only the wind whisking down Henley Street. My dream brought much contentment to my soul and I slept soundly until dawn. Later I told Judith about it. She is the only person I will ever tell, except you, my journal, my confidant, my preserver of hopes in a dusty world.

Stratford, June 29, 1597. Everyone likes our spring ale just fine. Grandfather even let me have a glass this year. He says I am a young lady now. And so I am.

Stratford, June 30, 1597. Perhaps Father wasn't so wrong when he said that I'd change my mind about these knaves we call boys. After all, some *are* interesting, at least from a distance.

Mother says that warm summer days will always turn a young heart to thoughts of love, and I should be careful of the attention I inspire. Yet the eyes of one Will Nash have kept me dreaming many a night. They are as black as the ink flowing from my pen. And three times as wild. But when I try to talk to him, he just babbles about nothing more exciting than cows and harvests and market wares. Froth and crows alive! What's wrong with this town?

Stratford, July 8, 1597. Horrible news! Richard Quiney, a neighbor who lives only two streets down from us, just returned from London with a report that my uncle Edmund has run afoul of the Master of Revels, a man named Tilney.

Mr. Quiney tried to calm us all, but his eyes betrayed him. Grandfather may have to leave for London soon to help sort this out. Father has specially requested Grandfather's help, as there are messages to be delivered in London that only a family member can be trusted with. Fortunately, Edmund's hearing has been scheduled for five days from now, so we have time to travel. I want to go. My uncles are too busy with the work in the shop, and Grandfather will need help. I will have to work on Mother for this one. Carefully, and without any yelling this time. Tilney, says Grandfather, has signed many a warrant that has clawed the bowels out of a man for nothing more than an ill-timed tavern jest at our queen and her ministers. Oh, Edmund, what have you done?

Two

"...in a cloud of smoke and books..."

Stratford, July 9, 1597. I haven't been able to sleep since hearing about Edmund's trouble. Grandfather said that Edmund had been arrested by Tilney for trying to rework and stage an old play about the Catholic martyr Sir Thomas More. Blasts and fogs! What was Edmund thinking? He knows how dangerous these days are for those of the old faith. I have a very bad feeling about this. But at least Mother has agreed to let me accompany Grandfather to London to help Father rescue Edmund. We must not lose hope, by my faith!

Stratford, July 10, 1597. We leave for London tomorrow. Judith and I went at dusk to the churchyard to pray for Edmund. In the midst of our prayers, Griffin Tallow's voice whispered to us through the iron gate.

"Susanna . . . I heard from my father that you're going to London," he said softly in the blue twilight. We joined him by the gate.

"Yes. Edmund's in serious trouble. Griffin, you must pray for us," I responded.

"I have something for you, to take on your trip." He handed me a small book, not much larger than my hand. It was bound in soft leather, and its gold-lined cover gleamed in the fading light.

"Is it a prayer book?" asked Judith.

"No, it's a work by Marsilio Ficino, an Italian, the most accomplished, holy, and revered scholar who ever charted the heavens. My father says the men in London who can open prisons at a mere word have their price. This is a fifteenth-century original, one of the many books that my father inherited from his uncle years ago. Take it to the booksellers at St. Paul's Cathedral. They'll pay you handsomely for it. You should be able to obtain enough money there to buy Edmund's safety. Though be careful—it's sometimes more a den of thieves than a church."

"Why are you giving us this?" asked Judith. "We can't possibly pay for it. And if our father can't, then Edmund certainly can't either."

"Don't worry about that," Griffin replied. "Your family has already paid for this book a long time ago."

"What are you talking about?" I asked.

"My father has told me how your grandfather helped mine out of terrible danger many years ago, when your grandfather was part of the town council. He saved his property from confiscation, and probably his life too. My father knows how valuable this book is, but he also knows how much we owe your family. Please take it in this time of need."

"Thank you, Griffin," I said, taking the book from his hand and pulling Judith in my direction. "We must go now. Pray for us!"

"I will!" Griffin said as we left him, a lonely scholar lean as the slender trees that hung over the graves of Swan Town's departed citizens. Judith laughed at his strange ways all the way home, but I held on to his book as if it were a sack of gold.

London, July 14, 1597. We have just arrived at Father's house, not too far from the theaters. As I write this, dawn has lit the eastern ridge of the city already. Steeples and chimneys thick as a field of wildflowers rise out of the darkness. It's a good thing Grandfather knows this huge city so well. His days as Swan Town's high bailiff brought him here yearly. After a warm hug from Father, I must sleep for a few hours.

Later. Edmund is being held under the jurisdiction of the City of London for attempting to rewrite *The Booke of Sir Thomas More,* a play cobbled together a few years ago by several London playwrights. Tilney, the Master of Revels, wrote that any company acting the play would do so "at their own peril." It seems there is too much sympathy in the play for More, a martyr for the old faith. Somehow, Edmund got the idea that if he were able to rework a scene or two, he might, like my father, land a spot writing for a company. Even Father tried to write up a scene or two a few years ago, yet it was still objectionable to Tilney. Knot-pated boy!

I don't know what we'll do. Tilney refuses any visitors.

Father spent two hours waiting for the Earl of Southampton without success. He says the earl has been a patron of his since his first days in London and swears he'll get an interview soon, and the means to help Uncle Edmund. Meanwhile, the twenty-two gallows on Tower Hill grow dark with ravens plucking at the remains of heretics and rebels.

It is so good to see Father, even in this dark time. I know he's worried about Edmund, as well as about a hundred other things. He's a whirlwind of activity, carrying the bundles of his own play scripts at all times, as if they were written on gold leaf. Good sooth, they almost are! They're worth more to me than that! He left Swan Town on the strength of such writings, the son of a glover, to become London's most popular playwright. With nothing more than a quill pen he has conquered a whole world of theaters and playing companies. He is a wonder. I pray he can work another kind of wonder for Edmund, and soon.

"If I can just speak with Southampton," said Father over a glass of ale, "I can convince him that this whole miserable business is a misunderstanding. I can't believe Edmund would be so reckless, I simply can't." He drummed his fingers nervously on the table. He knew better than most the stakes riding on the next few days. Yet his outward calm—except for those fingers!—reassured Grandfather and me.

"The Master of Revels is notorious for swift punishments," continued Father. "He knows how to keep his unruly playhouses in line. Time is worth more than gold now—it's worth Edmund's life."

London, July 16, 1597. While Father was off to see the Earl of Southampton, Grandfather and I spent the morning delivering messages, then went to a nearby market to buy some fruit and wine. On the way back, we saw a large crowd gathering around Tower Hill. Thousands seemed drawn to the place, as mindless moths are to a ghastly flame!

At first we didn't want to see, wanted anything but a view of the grisly business. But something, some force, pulled us closer too. Soon we found ourselves standing amid the large crowd of cobblers, shopkeepers, law students, grocers, mud-stained horse holders, and the like. Except for a low, constant murmur, all were quiet, as if in a church. All eyes strained for a look over the heads and shoulders in front, where the hooded executioners did their work. The smells of sweat and horse manure mixing with mud from a recent rain wrinkled my nose.

"What poor souls shall suffer this morning?" asked Grandfather in a low voice.

A man next to us, his doublet tattered and worn, overheard. "They're bringing out an entire household, they are. Accused of treasonous practices, you understand—coining, and hidin' priests. Not that I'd do so myself. But it's a shame, it is, since some in that family is younger than my two sons here."

As he said this, he put his hand on the shoulders of two boys, the oldest about my age, I gathered.

"Here they come!" someone shouted.

A procession of a sort came forth, flags flying in the light wind, pikes standing high over the heads of the crowd.

"We should leave," said Grandfather. "I don't want to see this, and neither do you."

"In a moment," I heard myself say. Perhaps I wanted to

make sure this was happening. Though seeing helpless Mrs. Smythe ducked for no reason at all was evil enough, this was an even worse horror. But here it was, happening with all the force and heraldry of law.

Like some strangely turbulent sea, the crowd suddenly parted and spread to the east and west, giving us a better view. The man was right. It was a family: a father and mother and their two children, a boy and a girl, both about my age. Maybe they were twins.

Amid the low murmuring of the crowd, a booming voice cried out: "Matthew and Martha Robinson . . . and you, Abigail and Richard Robinson . . . for false coining of Her Majesty's lawful currency . . . for harboring of outlawed priests of Romish treasons . . . and for other sundry felonies . . . shall be here hanged and drawn . . . your liver . . . your lungs . . . and entrails . . . from which your wicked thoughts proceed . . . shall be burned in boiling pitch . . . by the lawful pious code of Her Majesty's . . ."

What happened next is a blur, perhaps because of the swiftness of the executioners or the shock of seeing what I couldn't imagine really happening. In seconds the two adults were hanging from a scaffold. The man's pants darkened with urine, then he was let down. A flashing blade was in the air. His shirt was ripped off his back. A red stream shot out, then another. The crowd hissed at the disemboweling. His screams made my side teeth hurt. The world was narrowing down to total darkness, my heart pounding like a drum.

Edmund! God forbid that you appear before such monsters! After tugging on Grandfather's sleeve, I ran off, away from this scene of horror. I didn't stop until I came to the steps of Father's home, my clothes, even my face, splashed with mud.

After a few minutes Grandfather caught up, wheezing and coughing so much for breath that he made me sorry I had run ahead. He sat down beside me on the steps. After letting him rest a moment, I buried my head in his shoulder and sobbed.

"It's all right now, girl, for you must listen to me. You've seen the darkest that can be on this island, there's no doubt of that. But remember, as each seed within an apple is but an orchard unseen, so the martyr's blood will bloom with life, for us and for all in this dear troubled land. You must believe it."

"But those poor people! And Edmund? What if that happens to him? I couldn't bear it, I just couldn't!"

"Aye, that's why you must pray, and be strong."

London, July 17, 1597. Again, Father waited much of a day away with no result. This morning he was up before dawn, off again to wait for an audience with the Earl of Southampton, his former patron and potential savior of our dear Edmund. After lunch, when Grandfather took a nap, I decided to head for Ludgate Hill and the booksellers at St. Paul's. Since Grandfather might not believe that such a small thing could help with Edmund's release, I thought it best to try this sale on my own.

Carefully wrapping Griffin's book in my Coventry blue cloak, I walked down the crowded London streets, pretending I knew exactly where I was going. Thankfully, Griffin had drawn me a map (which he kindly had inserted in the book), and with its help, and two or three pointers from some helpful people on the street, I soon saw the cathedral looming up into the sky ahead of me.

What a sight! This great cathedral, built centuries before I was born, had become a marketplace, a byway of bawds, a scurvy-ridden, litter-filled ghost of a church. As I walked through the front entrance, I was met by tables filled with books, parchments, and maps; scriveners; arguing lawyers; addled messengers; and above them all a partially collapsed roof, occupied by fluttering pigeons that splashed their droppings on the mass of people below. Mother of fools! Is this what Her Majesty had let this church become? How sad, to see these bare, ruined choirs, marking no music but the sound of coins dropping into greedy hands and pockets.

Well, I wasn't about to let this place intimidate me.

I went over to where the booksellers bought and sold their goods. Books were piled high on tables, row upon row. Two or three chickens actually roamed about down the aisles, looking for a handout or a dropped hazelnut here and there. There seemed to be scores of conversations, deals, and such going on at the same time. One tallish man with fine new whiskers smiled at me as he examined some large volumes on a nearby table; otherwise, I was about as much noticed as the pigeons overhead.

Then a man with shaggy red hair and a pockmarked face caught my eye. As I got closer, I noticed that his filthy whiskers looked more like a rat's nest than a proper beard. Yet he seemed harmless enough, and he was the only buyer who wasn't busy, so I approached him with Griffin's book tucked under my arm.

"What have ye there, lass, something for sale?"

"Yes, it's a very rare volume," I answered, "and I'll sell it to you for the right price."

"And what might that be?" he shot back. "What experience do you have with the selling and buying of books?"

"Well, little really, but the friend who gave it to me said it was worth a great deal."

He looked to his right and left quickly and then asked to examine the book. I was a little unsure of what to do, but I knew I just had to get something to help Edmund. With an unsteady hand I put the volume down on the table in front of me.

The man's jagged left eyebrow rose a little and then quivered. He didn't touch the book right away; he just looked at the binding for what seemed a long time.

"What do you think?" I asked.

He picked it up and then almost carelessly fanned the pages, looking quickly at the inside front cover. Then in a blur he tucked it under his arm and looked me in the eye.

"It's not worth three shillings, but as you're a well-brought-up young lass, I'll give you four for it."

"Four shillings!" I said, shocked. "You must be joking. This book's worth a hundred times that, I am sure of it."

He moved back a step or two when he heard this, clearly irritated.

"Listen, lass, this book isn't worth that in this life or the next—in fact, I'd say that it looks just like the one someone pocketed from my stall last week. I've been looking for it all over, I have. So begone with you! And count yourself lucky I don't take this to the law. Begone, I say!"

Before I could recover from my shock, he slammed his stall

sign down so it said CLOSED, and dashed off behind the stacks, lost amid hundreds of books and those wandering chickens. I felt like someone had kicked me in the stomach. Yet, remembering that Edmund's life might well depend on the money I could gain from Griffin's book, I gathered my wits and sprang into action. I wasn't about to let this flea-bitten rag of a man steal our chance at saving Edmund.

"Foul knave! You have no right to that book! Stop!"

This was no time for bashfulness. I gathered up the hem of my dress, jumped over his table, and ran into the stacks and piles of dusty books that formed the maze into which the pocked villain had fled. He seemed to have vanished. I slowed down and looked around, listening. Then, to my right, I suddenly heard someone wheezing. Taking three steps in that direction, I looked down an aisle of stacked boxes and books and there saw my bookseller, crouched in a corner, holding a pistol, its ugly black mouth aimed directly at me. Griffin's book was in his lap.

I could hear the crowds milling about around us, oblivious to the drama taking place within the crowded cathedral.

"Now, girl," he said in a low, scratchy voice, "if you know what's good for you, you'll just back off slowly and walk out of here as if we'd never met. Hear me, lass?"

I took a deep breath and looked right into his bloodshot eyes.

"Sir, that is my book, and I'll not leave here without it."

"Arrant girl, that's not the right answer." As he said this, he used both hands to cock his pistol, then leveled it at my head. All I could think of was Edmund, and the clock running down to his terrible fate before Tilney's court. I took a step forward.

Then the world suddenly seemed to explode in a cloud of smoke and books.

For a moment there was only a tremendous ringing in my ears, greater than if I had been stuck inside one of the huge bells of a London church and left to chime the hours. Smoke stung my eyes. As it cleared, I could see the arms and legs of the foul bookseller sticking out of a huge pile of books. Something or someone had thrown a whole shelf of reading right on top of him! Then a strong, concerned voice rang out: "My goodness! Are you all right? I had to act fast, and that was the only thing I could think to do! I hope you're not hurt."

Turning around, I saw the young man with the fine whiskers who had smiled at me as I had approached the book tables. His eyes were as blue as cornflowers. Though I felt a little weak in the knees, I otherwise seemed unhurt.

"Thank you, I'm fine, or at least I think I am. What in God's name happened?"

"I saw your friend here giving you trouble and followed you into the stacks. By the time I saw him raise that cannon of his, I knew I had to act as quickly as possible. So I dumped a whole crate of books on his head and hoped for the best."

As he said this, Red-beard started to groan, and tried to push off the mountain of learning that lay on top of him. He appeared twice as stunned as I was by the sudden avalanche.

"Look, we'd better get out of here," said the man who had saved me. "He'll be up in a minute or two, and twice as nasty. Follow me."

Red-beard's shot had certainly gotten the attention of everyone in the cathedral. A few loud voices began to call for the constable to bring some order to the place, while another yelled for some rope and a group of men to help him search the stacks. I had to get out of here. But bolts and shackles! I couldn't forget about Edmund! So with one quick swoop down at the pile of books, I fished out Griffin's volume and joined my newfound friend as he led the way out of this temple given over to the gods of thievery and gold.

Once we were a few blocks from the cathedral (with Griffin's book held tightly under my arm), I stopped and looked at this man who had just saved my life.

"Well," I said, blushing slightly, "I suppose we should introduce ourselves."

"My name is John Hall," he said with a slight bow. He had gentle eyes such as I had never seen, yet strong, too. For some reason I felt a little flutter in my stomach. What was I afraid of? Tallow-catch! This was beyond my figuring.

"My name is Susanna Shakespeare," I said with a slight curtsy. He squinted at my last name, as if he recognized it. Before I could say anything about my father, he asked, "Is your father the famous writer from Warwickshire . . ."

"He is indeed," I said proudly.

"Yes, I thought so—the tracts he's written on colic and purgatives are the best I've ever read!"

What was he talking about?

"My father writes plays. And poetry."

He looked confused. "Oh, I thought Robert Shakespeare wrote solely on medical topics. Well, that just shows what a well-rounded man he is. I would love to meet him sometime."

"My father's name is William. He writes for the theaters in London. He's played before the queen, in fact."

"I'm sorry, I didn't know. My fellow students are always

trying to coax me into coming with them to the theaters here. Now how I will dodge them?" he said with a smile. "May I ask where you are from? Not around here, I gather."

"No, I live in Stratford, with my grandparents, my sister, and our mother."

We walked another minute or so in awkward silence. The sound of horses and coaches clattering on cobblestones echoed all around us. The sound of a busy city, full of strangers, thieves, and violent booksellers.

It suddenly struck me how close I had come to being killed, had it not been for the kindness of this stranger. Griffin's book must be worth quite a ransom if that bookseller felt it worth shooting someone over.

"I can't believe I'm still in one piece. How can I ever thank you?"

"No need, really. My pleasure," he said with a slight bow.

"I'll never be able to thank you enough, but right now I need to get back to my grandfather and meet my father. You see, this book is our only hope."

"It must be a very special book."

I thought quickly. Perhaps John could be of further assistance. "You said you are a student?"

"At Cambridge. I study medicine. That's why I was in St. Paul's. I am always looking for more books to help me in my studies."

One thing was certain: I needed to sell this book and get back to Father as soon as possible. Maybe here was my chance.

"It looks as if I need your help once again. I need to turn this book into money, as quickly as possible. Could you help me sell it, so I can help my father win his brother's release from prison? He's a player at one of the theaters, and now he's going before the Master of Revels on some terrible misunderstanding that could cost him his life. I must help him before it's too late."

"May I see the book?" John asked.

"Certainly," I said, taking it out of my cloak. He examined it quickly and handed it back to me.

"I recognize the author, but I'm no judge of rare books. It's getting late—we certainly can't go back to St. Paul's, not after all that. Show that book to whoever can free your uncle and tell them you'll be able to sell it tomorrow. I know a bookseller on the other side of the city who will give you an honest price for it. He's too far away for us to try now, and he usually closes shop right about this hour. But if that book's as valuable as our bookseller here thought it was, you'll get fair money for it tomorrow, I assure you."

Looking at the sun dipping below the buildings in the west, I knew he was right. I'd have to chance the few hours' delay in getting any kind of payment for releasing Edmund. It was the only hope we had left, at any rate.

"You're very kind, Mr. Hall. Where shall we meet tomorrow?"

"Tell your father I'll be at the Brockley Jack, a tavern by Pasternoster Row, in the early afternoon."

"I will! Thank you!"

"The pleasure is all mine, Miss Shakespeare. And so till we meet again."

"Yes, until then."

Later. Father was already back from the Earl of Southampton's home when I returned. His lordship's servants had assured him that their master would be in that evening. Grandfather and I were supposed to wait here, while Father and his fellow players John Heminges and Henry Condell went to the earl's estate. What! How could I stay behind? Father had some money available but was mainly relying on his friendship with the earl to gain Edmund's freedom. What if that wasn't enough?

Unfortunately, I also felt that now wasn't the time to tell Father about Griffin's gift or John's favor. Everything was just too complicated, and events were moving quickly. And for all I knew, as much as Father wanted to save Edmund, he might not like me getting involved in something like this. If I was going to help, it would have to be when Father couldn't possibly refuse. But I simply had to go with him, or my hope of helping Edmund would come to nothing.

"It's too dangerous," replied Father when I asked. "You'd be out of place, and besides, we don't want to do anything to upset the earl. He's our only hope. You can keep your Grandfather company, even wait up for us, if you like. But you must stay here."

I recognized the tone in his voice. He was more tired and worried than any of us. Clever now, I thought. Don't make it worse.

"Father, you know I'd never do anything to hurt our chances of getting Edmund freed, but I must come with you. He'd do the same for me, if I were in trouble."

"But you're not," said Father, while packing a leather pouch with some books.

I looked over at Heminges and Condell for support, but their eyes told me this was my own fight. They worked with

Father, and knew as well as I that he could be both the kindest and most stubborn of men. And of course Grandfather would never publicly take my side against Father.

"But I was!" I continued. "Remember when some traveling players came to Stratford a few months ago, and Judith and I were almost kidnapped by those roving fiends?"

"Your mother mentioned it—just some players having some fun, hardly worth talking about, I thought."

"Not for Judith and me! Who knows what would have happened if Edmund hadn't helped us! Those men were capable of making us servants for life, and that's no lie."

"How did he get involved with that? His troupe didn't go to Stratford."

"Yes it did, but he promised not to tell you so we wouldn't get into any more trouble. Edmund risked damaging his stage career—his dream—to save us, and look how you want me to repay him! I can't stay here, don't you *understand*? I've seen Tower Hill. I've seen what could happen to Edmund with my own eyes."

Father's face showed me I had made my point. I turned away from him, to gather my thoughts and keep from crying. This was too important for tears.

"My dear," he said, "I love you more than anything, but you must understand. This is too important for a young girl. I need not tell you that Edmund's life depends on the impression our petition makes with the earl. I just can't risk your coming along. The matter is settled."

Maddening obstacle! The very moment I thought I had him pinned with the overwhelming logic of my case, he slipped free quicker than a morsel of greasy mutton! And that remark about being too young, and a girl? How galling! What was he expecting me to do, knit by the fire until he returned? But lean-witted fool that I am, there was no answering his arguments, at least not at the moment. This was his final word—I could see that.

Father kissed me once, and grabbed his cloak and satchel. "Heminges, Condell," he said, "let's go! Time to take the first ferry we see, and hope his lordship is open to saving a player's life tonight."

And then they were gone, with Grandfather half asleep by the fire and Griffin's book sitting uselessly under my cloak. Hound of Crete! My head felt like bursting at the thought of losing Edmund because my father wouldn't trust a girl my age. What knavish ideas fathers toss about their brains, especially when it comes to judging daughters!

I had to move fast. Grandfather was now asleep, an empty cup of ale on the table by his elbow, his regular snores serenading the quiet hearth. Blasts and fogs! It was now or never! Since I couldn't navigate the London streets at night by myself, I needed to follow Father and his friends secretly— and on their very heels. But I needed to disguise myself first. A costume of some sort, to prevent Father from seeing me as I followed.

Several feathered hats were hanging by the door, as well as three doublets. One of the velvet doublets was almost my size, and when I put it on over my bodice, it fitted fine. Some willow-green breeches that I found in Father's bedroom also fit, though I had to roll up the cuffs and pin the waist a few inches in. On the way out I grabbed one of the hats, a beautiful Bristol red, with a yellow feather flowing on its right side.

Several twists of my braids and a tuck inside my hat, and I was ready to go. With luck I could follow Father to his lordship's estate and be waiting with Griffin's book, should an opportunity present itself.

Father's remark to his fellow players about taking a ferry told me that the Southampton estate must be on the other side of the Thames. Since there were scores of wherrymen by the riverbank waiting for passengers at any given moment of the day or night, I had to catch up with them quickly if I was to see which boat they took and gain the other shore in time to follow them.

After running as fast as I could down our street in the direction of the river, I spied Father and Heminges and Condell taking a right onto the next street. At the same moment, I put my foot squarely into a pile of horse droppings and nearly slipped onto the jagged cobblestones, filthy with muck and mire. Bean-fed horses! Luckily, I kept myself from hitting the ground by grabbing hold of a stone post that marked where the street began and sidewalk and gutter ended. Another slip like that and I'd never make it into his lordship's hall. Not smelling like a stable boy, that was certain!

When I arrived at the river, Father and his friends were aboard a ferry and beginning to push off for the other bank. Looking about me, I saw the Thames curving around the city like a broad band of black velvet, studded with winking stars and wherrymen's lanterns lighting their way to the opposite shore. The foul smell of rotting fish seemed to rise up out of the river muck, and the dark water slapped against the line of docks that ran as far as the eye could see.

After asking the nearest wherryman his fare, I flipped him

his payment and began climbing into his ferry. He was wrapped in heavy scarves about the face and shoulders, so I couldn't get a sense of what he was like, but his voice was reassuring enough. "Get in, lad," he said, "and I'll get ya across the riva 'fore you can say Thames and back agin."

"Thank you," I said in a low voice, while taking my seat in the back of his boat and keeping my eye on Father's ferry not a hundred paces ahead of us. My rower must have been particularly strong, because before I knew it, we were gaining on Father at an alarming rate. We were getting so close! Looking back at my ferryman, who was sitting in the center of the boat, I said, again in a low voice, "I'm in no particular rush, sir, as long we make it safely to the other side." But like some phantom bent on making the farther shore, he seemed oblivious to anything but his rowing.

Cold spray from the lapping current on the river sent a shiver through me, but there was nothing I could do now except hold on. With a quick tug on my hat to make sure it wouldn't fly off in the wind, I looked away from Father's ferry, some thirty paces to my right, hoping that my disguise and the darkness would hide me. I could feel our ferry surge ahead, and out of the corner of my eye even noticed we were side by side with Father for a whole pulse-stopping minute! I didn't dare look straight in their direction, though I distinctly heard Father's voice, and then a laugh or two from his friends. And then, thank God, we rowed past his boat and actually reached the docks a moment or two before they did. Jackanapes with scarves! I did it! I sailed right by them, and they didn't notice me in the least! My heart pounded with excitement at the thought of outwitting my father—so far, anyway.

"Here ya are, lad," said my rower, suddenly showing an ability to speak again. "May ya prosper here, and gain the other shore safely, come what may."

"Thank you, sir," I said, as I mingled into the crowds awaiting a ferry and the new arrivals like myself. All the while, of course, I kept a keen eye on Father. He and his fellow players leaped confidently out of their ferry and quickly made their way from the docks into the darkened streets of London, north of the river. I followed, trying all the while not to come too close or lag so far behind that I might lose them in the crowd. If I lost them here, I'd sooner find my way out of a labyrinth than find my way to the Southampton estate.

I dodged around corners strewn with trash, ran by boys selling chestnuts roasting on their street-side coal fires, and passed drunken fools quarreling over games of dice. I followed Father and his friends for more than two miles, and still they kept on. I never imagined that London would be so busy at night, but here it was, humming with life beneath a sky filled with glittering stars and a quarter moon. Remembering that Griffin's book was in a leather satchel over my shoulder, I gave it a reassuring squeeze to make sure it was still safe, and pushed on.

Finally it looked as if we had reached our destination. The Southampton estate was huge, easily the size of a whole street of houses back in Swan Town. An open gate, with a sleepy guard on a bench, led to a cobblestone drive that stretched to the main house. The mansion had what seemed like hundreds of windows on three levels, though only the upper floors were lit with candles. I followed closely now, barely twenty paces away. Thankfully, there were enough servants going back and forth for me to remain unnoticed. Father clearly knew his way around, for he walked without hesitation to the central great hall and asked for his lordship's secretary.

Once inside the hall, I found the darkened nook of a window in which to hide and watch. Soon a man in a dark doublet and ruff approached Father and his friends in front of the huge fireplace. Some conversation passed between them, but I couldn't make it out. Then I distinctly heard Father say "Thank you," and as the man departed, Father and Heminges and Condell sat before the fire. I luckily found a shelf in my nook to sit on, which made my wait a little easier, though a draft from the window made me envious of the warmth they enjoyed by the crackling hearth.

A chillier, draftier hall than that belonging to the Earl of Southampton doesn't exist in all of England, if you ask me. I don't remember such a cold and damp July ever before. I tried to read a page or two from the book Griffin gave me, but in the darkened corner I couldn't make out very much. The hours passed slowly. Heminges and Condell fell asleep by the fire. With a peek or two out of my nook, I realized only Father and I remained awake, listening to the creaking of the hall rafters as the night gnawed away at Edmund's chances for escape. How I longed to make my presence known to him, but I didn't dare. Not yet.

Finally, Heminges woke up, and started talking with Father. My footsteps were quieter than a dormouse as I crept closer until I found another window nook draped in shadow and stood and listened. In the silence of the empty hall, I could hear every word.

"You know," said Father, "I'd give it all up just to save Edmund."

"Give what up?" asked Heminges.

"My work in the theater, my acting, my writing even. What use is a gift if it tears your world apart? Edmund is worth more than a century of plays to me."

Heminges smiled and put his hand on Father's shoulder. "You know, this isn't the first time a player of ours needed help, and it won't be the last, I daresay. Don't you worry about Edmund—he's made of the same stuff as you are, I can tell. He'll get through, he will."

Father looked up. "I hope you're right, because if he doesn't, there will be no second act for Edmund tonight. His curtain will fall. Tilney will see to that."

A pox on that thought! How could he say such a thing?

A heavy door suddenly slammed shut. Dogs howled outside the main gate, followed by the sound of horses crossing cobblestones.

Father jumped up while Heminges woke Condell, and both followed Father to meet the arriving Earl of Southampton and his companion. Servants had just stoked up the fire with fresh logs and tinder. The older man walked with a slight limp, while the younger man carried himself with a certain grace found, I imagine, only in those born to great wealth and power.

As they made their introductions, I slipped two window nooks closer to better hear. The older man, I discovered, was the Earl of Oxford, a rakish-looking fellow if there ever was one. He seemed to admire my father, judging by the tone of his remarks. I watched from the flickering shadows as the most important performance of Father's life began.

"Your lordships," said Father with a neat, observant bow,

"please forgive this intrusion at so late an hour, but I need some immediate assistance in a matter dearer to my heart than words can say."

"Well, Will, if you can't find words for the matter, it must be something pressing indeed," said Southampton, setting his riding crop on a table near the fire as he turned attentively to his player friend.

"To be brief, my lord, my brother Edmund has been arrested by order of Master Tilney."

"The reason?" asked Southampton, signaling Oxford to sit as servants brought drinks.

"An old play, my lord. Edmund thought he might rework *The Booke of Sir Thomas More*, even after Tilney pronounced it unplayable."

"Nothing like those old martyrs to get Londoners all frothy, Henry," remarked Oxford with a laugh.

Southampton let out a sigh. His young face glowed in the firelight. He gave Oxford a knowing look, as if they had already agreed beforehand on the outcome of this drama.

"Tilney is responsible to the lord chamberlain," said Southampton, "and the lord chamberlain is answerable to Her Majesty. It's that simple, Will. This might sound like a little incident, but if I meddle in this decision, it could hurt my standing with the queen. Her Majesty controls the flow of taxes in this realm, and her displeasure can lower the profit I earn from my properties. I'm sorry, but there's nothing we can do."

"But he is young, and new to the playhouses—"

"There's the pity of it," said Southampton. "Our playhouses have been the ruin of many a young man. I don't need to tell you that."

"What could I offer in exchange?" asked Father, his voice getting desperate. "A new play? A share in the theater?"

Oxford sat up at the last offer and tried to get Southampton's eye. The young earl kept looking into the fire, right past my father, as if he weren't there.

"I'm terribly sorry, Will. Even your plays, the most applauded in this city, couldn't raise the kind of income I'd put at risk by interfering with Tilney," said Southampton.

I could see Father was losing this battle, and quickly. These two powerful men would use their influence only in their own self-interest. It was as plain as day. Griffin's book was in my hand now, and it was time to raise the stakes, of that I was sure. Would it really be worth its weight in sterling? Would it be worth a glover's son, a would-be playwright and sometime actor?

There was only one way to know. After taking off my hat and shaking out my hair, I stepped out of the shadows, my footsteps echoing in the large hall as I walked over to the men. The raftered ceiling seemed hundreds of feet over my head.

"Pardon me, your lordships," I said with a curtsy, "but I believe I have just the thing to persuade you to save that poor player, my uncle Edmund."

"Susanna! What are you doing here?" cried Father.

"And who might you be?" asked Southampton, with a hint of curiosity in his voice.

"I am sorry, my lord. This is my elder daughter, Susanna, someone I thought had learned the value of obedience, especially to her father."

"Father, let me show them—"

"No! Now go back to the front entrance, and stay there. I won't be long."

"Please!"

Before he could answer, Oxford spoke up.

"Now, lass, what do you think worth a player who winds up in Newgate, guilty of offending our Master of Revels?"

"A book. A very valuable one, your lordship, one that I could sell tomorrow morning for fifty pounds, delivered directly to you. Unless, that is, you are interested in old books yourself."

"How old?" asked Southampton, showing sudden interest at the new turn of events.

"Well, let's see," I said, opening the cover, "It says 1489. Is that old enough?"

"Let me see it," said Southampton, taking it out of my hands. He held it close to his face and turned the pages. A stick in the fire popped and cracked. No one said anything. Father looked at me with a mixture of puzzlement and anger, as if I had temporarily lost my mind, or worse. Southampton suddenly gasped.

"My God, Edward! This is a first edition of Ficino's *The Three Books of Life*. He's the marvelous Italian who has mapped the harmonies of the whole universe, the great Chain of Being itself. I have heard of this book but have never seen one, much less been able to buy it for my library. I must have it. You must sell it to me!"

"Remember what it will cost you," said Oxford dryly, picking some dried mud off his boot.

"I would exchange a whole company of players for this one Italian, even sell one of my estates if I had to!"

"I thought you said it was impossible for you to lose that kind of income," said Oxford.

"I hardly reckoned on such an opportunity, Edward," answered Southampton, regaining his composure. He turned to me. "Where did you get this?"

"In Stratford. A friend gave it to me," I said, hardly able to believe my good luck.

"Well, Miss Shakespeare. I will trade this volume for your actor uncle. Do you consider it a fair exchange?"

"A most fair one, your lordship," I said.

"Despite her forwardness, she's well brought up, Will. I can see she gets her wits from you."

"And her mother, your lordship—they are both most clever beauties, if I may say so," answered Father, relieved and now almost smiling.

"You certainly may, for she's saved your brother's life!"

Southampton rose from his chair. Father bowed, and I curtsied again, this time with a more sincere heart, God knows! Oxford remained sitting, his thoughts elsewhere.

"William, go to Newgate at dawn. Your brother will be waiting for you to take him home."

"Your lordship, how can I ever thank you?" asked Father bowing.

"Stay away from those old More plays, will you?" came the answer, quicker than a shooting star. "And if you don't get that daughter of yours a tutor, at least make sure she marries a man who can share his learning. A brave heart needs a lettered mind."

London, July 18, 1597. Just as the hundreds of London church bells chimed in the early morning, Uncle Edmund walked out of prison, a free man. How good it was to see him, safe at last! Holy Lazarus! Was he ever a lucky one!

Earlier, as we left the Southampton's estate, Father's face expressed the most incredible mixture of surprise, relief, and anger I have seen in my life! Though when he put his arm around me and gave me a hug, I knew which emotions had won out. I immediately told him about how I got Griffin's book, then almost lost it, and my life, at the cathedral, in my battle with the red-bearded bookseller and his pistol. How I would be dead except for this John Hall, of Cambridge, who will surely be waiting to meet me today at the Brockley Jack, where we must all go to thank him. When I finished, somewhat breathless, Father smiled and hugged me again.

"I must meet this fellow," he said. "Let's go to the Brockley Jack, just as you said, and thank Mr. Hall for his kindness."

By my troth! Somehow, as much as I wanted to see John again, I just didn't know what to make of our sudden meeting. I must stop such silliness and simply thank him and be done with it. Our meeting was just a lucky chance for me, and thank God it was. One curtsy to John Hall, and then back to Swan Town. I'd had my fill of this magical, dangerous city, I had! At least for now.

Later. About noon, we all set out for the Brockley Jack. Grandfather and Edmund were in high spirits—Edmund knew of the tavern as one of the better places to get a good dinner—though Father and I were quiet, lost in our own thoughts. What was I supposed to say to John, besides thank you? I hardly noticed the brilliant blue sky overhead, or how the river shone like silver even with the smelly streams of garbage flowing into it.

"Here we are," said Edmund, holding open the door,

above which hung a sign with a twisted little pirate leaning on a ship's mast. The pirate was caught in the act of winking his left eye, as if sharing a private joke with every guest who passed through Brockley Jack's doors.

The tavern was fairly crowded, and in its two fireplaces small smoldering fires burned. John was seated at a table by himself. He stood up when he saw me and waved us over.

"I am so glad to see you, Miss Shakespeare," he said. "My bookseller friend will offer you a handsome price today—a player's ransom, I am sure."

"Thank you for your help yesterday, Mr. Hall," I began nervously. "But we don't need any booksellers today. If you please, let me introduce everybody before I explain. This is my father, William, and my grandfather, John Shakespeare, and finally the one we've worried over these last few days, my uncle Edmund."

John smiled and shook hands with them all, and then invited us to sit for a drink. Before long, it seemed as if we had known each other for quite some time. When I explained that Southampton had turned out to be a collector of old books, and had been eager to own Griffin's book, we all laughed at our good luck. Edmund, of course, was especially grateful, and thanked John gallantly.

John's version of my encounter with the bookseller at first entranced everyone with its danger and suspense; then his account of the roar of the pistol and the falling books had us all laughing and wondering at how everything had worked out so miraculously well.

Even sitting next to my beloved uncle, safe at last, and my father, I found myself glancing at John often. Saying good-bye to him was not the trifle I had expected it to be. God's lid! Something was happening, something I had not experienced before in all my life. How could I feel this way, and just watch John Hall, to whom I owed my life, walk out of there, never to see him again? A final thank-you, and that's it?

"Now tell me, young Hall," Father suddenly demanded. "Susanna says you've never visited one of our playhouses before. Well, we'll have to remedy that, for you are certainly welcome at the Swan anytime, compliments of Will Shakespeare. Just tell them at the door, and you'll be shown the best seat in the house, I promise."

"That's very kind of you, Mr. Shakespeare," answered John. "But I am a Puritan, and so don't think the public theaters are a place I belong. I hope you understand."

A Puritan! Tedious stumbling block! Have I become taken with a Montague? Must I play a wretched Capulet, and not on some wooden stage but in my own life? I looked around me to see what reaction John's declaration had made on my family. Father's face flushed a shade or two darker, and he looked at Edmund for a moment. Grandfather cut in, saying: "Will perfectly understands, don't ye, Will? This boy's done enough for us to not worry over his Puritan leanings, hasn't he?"

"Of course he has," said Father. "Though it's a strange world that has such generous Puritans in it. But then, judge the man before you judge his creed, I always say." I wondered just what kind of Puritan John was. He couldn't be the darker sort, not after everything he had done for us, and for me.

At last it was time to be on our way. John shook hands with everyone, and then, for a few brief minutes, I was left alone with him while Father paid the bill and Edmund and

Grandfather made their way outside.

"I had no idea you were a Puritan," I blurted out.

"Well, I'm probably the most lighthearted Puritan on this whole island, at least after meeting you!"

A serving maid accidentally dropped a pint of ale on the floor behind us, and the crash made me jump. John took a step closer and held both my hands in his. They felt agreeably warm and firm holding mine.

"If you'd like, I could visit you in Stratford sometime, when my studies allow, of course."

"I would like that very much," I said after a moment.

Then I was off, joining Edmund, Father, and Grandfather as we made our way back to Father's house. Though I could feel my cheeks blushing, no one asked me what John and I had spoken of during our good-byes. Edmund put his arm around me as we walked.

"He's a right merry one for a Puritan," joked Grandfather. "When he's a doctor, maybe he could find a purge for that unfortunate Puritanism of his! Though it would be a scalding purge, it would!"

"Yes," laughed Father. "Though most Puritans, I find, hold on to their gall as if it were gold."

I laughed too, but God knows, my heart wasn't in it. Will John really visit me in Swan Town? What will I say if he does? O wit of the world and heaven above, grant me the right words to greet John Hall should he ever walk into my life again. This I pray.

Three

" . . . O treason of the blood!"

Stratford, July 22, 1597. How much has changed in just a few short days. Edmund was on the brink of disaster and is now safe again, working with Father at the Swan. John Hall, after saving my life, is back in Cambridge studying medicine, his promise to visit me lodged in my heart. The days here in Swan Town go on as always, tinkling cow bells counting the hours. Father says life is one big rehearsal except that the script we follow is our own, for better or worse. It is the worse I worry about, of course.

Leaving Father and Edmund in London was difficult, but the pain of that parting was lessened by the joy of meeting Mother and Judith and my other uncles with the news of Edmund's release from the shadow of death. They all laughed when I told how Grandfather wrapped Uncle Edmund in a giant hug and wouldn't let him go for several minutes.

"Oh my boy! I'll never speak ill of another book as long as I live . . . that I can tell you!" Grandfather had shouted. "I need to go find Griffin Tallow's father and buy him a pint of ale, I do. And that son of his! Why, I'll buy him a bushel of licorice, I will!"

I told everyone that Edmund seemed humbled by the whole experience. He said he should have known better than to try his hand at a play rich in old piety but lacking in wit. "The stage is not the place for direct jabs at the powers of this kingdom," he told us. "It takes a rapier, not a battering ram, to write for the stage safely these days, as Will well knows." God's shield! That's a truth I shall try to remember!

Later Edmund and I shared a special moment. We were walking side by side down a London street (how I had hoped for a moment like this, and now it was better than I ever imagined) when Edmund softly said to me: "Well, Susanna, I guess one good turn deserves another. Now I am in your debt. Though I doubt I could ever repay you with something as rare as that book Griffin Tallow gave you! And that friend of yours, John. A good fellow, despite his Puritanism. I do hope we see him again."

Villain Hall! How you haunt my days and nights! There's only one way to wait for you, and that's to bury myself in the soft, slow hours of this little town until you decide to visit. And then what? Who knows, for that water has yet to run under Clopton Bridge.

Stratford, July 23, 1597. After my experience in London— after seeing what Her Majesty's laws almost did to Edmund— I am beginning to think my play is not such a good idea. I have seen with my own eyes that there are people on this island with hearts harder than the forged iron with which they torture the innocent. Even a beef-wit should realize that a confrontation with the authorities who watch the theaters can mean disaster.

In fact, I have come to this conclusion with Judith's help, of all people. After sharing my adventures in London with Judith the other day, I also showed her the pages of my play and told her of my hope to someday see it performed, if only briefly, on Father's stage. Well, that valiant flea of a sister tried to take the pages from my hand and throw them into the fire. I rescued them and folded them safely away in my desk's secret panel. Even in light of the horror I had witnessed in London, I didn't want to admit she had a point. At least not right away, and without exacting a promise.

"How can you even think of such a thing, after what almost happened to Edmund?" asked Judith, lying on the bed, staring up at the sharply angled ceiling.

"Edmund admits that what he did was reckless," I said, "but my play is different from the piece he tried to work with, and much shorter too. But perhaps it is too dangerous to attempt such things these days. I've learned Tilney's not a man to be trifled with."

"Then you'll get rid of your play? Throw it in the fire?"

"I can't run about like some hare, afraid of my own heartbeat. But I'll promise to put it aside, if you'll agree to one thing."

"Which is?"

"That someday if I can perform a brief piece for Father's stage, safely and using plenty of side-glancing wit, of course, you will help me, even if it means going on the stage with me!"

"I can't imagine anything like that ever happening," said Judith.

"I learned quite a bit during my visit to London. Tilney and his kind don't care what the players do on the stage, so long as it's not inciting riots or praising martyrs of the old faith. One of these days, Judith, I just know it, I'll get my chance to show Father and Edmund I am more than just a young girl in tired old Swan Town. I've already gotten them out of one scrape as it is. With time and luck, there's no saying what I could do. But I need your help. Promise me. I won't work on my play until this incident with Edmund is long forgotten, and when I do, it won't have a single line mentioning the queen's religion, I promise."

Judith sat up and looked me in the eye.

"All right. When players can do as they like on London stages, you can count on my help. Until then, let's have nothing to do with plays that will get us into trouble. Agreed?"

"Agreed," I said. Judith soon went downstairs, leaving me alone with my quills and paper at my desk. The room felt stuffy and I opened the window near my desk. As I did, a mourning dove fluttered away from the ledge. The clean smell of a bunch of rosemary hanging by the window caught an incoming breeze. Its fragrance washed over me and made me remember why I had started writing in the first place. I needed this journal and even my play to shape my own life, and not be molded by the foolishness of others. If Judith didn't understand that, well, that was fine with me. But I would remember her promise, and if the times smiled on my hopes, I would make her remember it too.

But for now, she was right. It's time for my *Parrot King* to sleep. He may need the energy one day, I hope.

Stratford, July 24, 1597. Judith and I went over late in the day to see Griffin Tallow to thank him in person for his book. He had already received word of Edmund's safety and our thanks from Mother yesterday. Mrs. Tallow led us to the stairway leading to Griffin's room, with promise of some refreshment before we left.

Griffin's room, which he shared with his two younger brothers, was large and crammed full of books. Everywhere we looked was evidence of Griffin's interest in astrology and music and learning. Charts, astrolabes, and assorted parchments and maps littered the shelves and his desk, which looked out on the river.

"What did I tell you? That Ficino is a rare book," said Griffin, chewing on some of the licorice that Grandfather had given him. "No bookseller in London would pass it by, for within that volume you can discover the secrets of every planet and star and metal and stone that exerts its influence over this world of ours. It's no wonder the earl couldn't resist it."

"It was like offering a mouse half a barrel of cheese," I said.

"No doubt," said Griffin. "Ficino's quite a rarity. According to him, our lives themselves can become works of art, with the same harmonies that move the sun and the stars. And without love, Ficino thinks, we have about as much chance of making music as a lute without strings. Would you like a string of licorice?"

Stratford, August 1, 1597. Father is here on a surprise visit that has us all very excited. It seems that we are soon to move to our own house.

Father says business in London is getting better every

week, and has given him enough money for such a purchase. Judith and I can hardly wait to see it. Father said that negotiations were moving rather quickly, and we should start packing our belongings now. He is a bundle of activity, I swear! I don't see how he balances all those plays and poems and theater business within that balding pate of his!

After sunset, I went with Mother and Father to a barn some two miles north of Swan Town. For the first time in weeks, we heard mass, and Father helped me with the Latin. The priest seemed a very devout man. I couldn't help staring at his whiskers, which were as thick as a mule's tail.

Stratford, August 3, 1597. Father is nearly finished with the details of the contract for purchasing New Place at the corner of Chapel Street and Chapel Lane. The house is splendid.

According to Father (I have my own sources too), it has a story: The house was built by Hugh Clopton, Stratford's most generous son. This same Clopton built our best bridge, its stones firmly flung across the Avon since before my father was born.

In 1563, a descendent of his decided to sell New Place to a William Bott, a man later charged with various and wicked crimes. It's even said he poisoned his own daughter to gain more land for himself, based on an agreement taken out in her name. According to an eyewitness, the poor girl swelled all over her body, and her skin turned scarlet in great blotches. She died shortly thereafter, a victim to her family's greedy desire for land. Mere earth.

These horrors occurred at New Place. I asked Father if he was troubled by the house's shadowy past.

He said he thought it would help him write.

Stratford, August 9, 1597. Today we moved into our new house! It's very, very exciting. Neither Judith nor I can sleep. If only Hamnet were here. He'd love to prance about and explore every nook of this magnificent place. Our house has *five* gables, three floors, a beautiful courtyard, two barns, and two orchards, though the latter need much work before they're anything to boast of. There are three hidden rooms that I know about so far: one above and to the right of the kitchen; a second in back of my bedroom; and a third near the upper guest room, street side. I suspect there are more. The one above the kitchen shall be mine alone: Judith says she doesn't like small, windowless places. I take what privacy I can get, even if I do have to share it with spiders.

Father says he wants to plant vines in the orchard and a mulberry tree in what he called "the Great Garden." Well, it's not so great now, but in time, with Father's eye for planting, it will be. We are lucky to live in such a house. God has been good to us of late.

Stratford, August 11, 1597. We are so happy in our new house, and after all the work we've done, we should be. A bedroom in the southeast side of the house had strange stains splashed over the walls. The windows in back were cracked, the attic spaces harbored more spiders than I could count (more even than in my secret room!). Many of the rooms are still in need of replastering, however, and in some cases require completely new beams and hardware on the windows and doors. Large sections of basement stone are also missing, leaving gaps by which rain gained easy entrance. I also found a pile of animal bones under the loose boards in the kitchen floor . But now it is a fine, goodly place. Even with its shadows and secrets.

Stratford, August 12, 1597. Last night, we had a most enjoyable time, for Father's friends Ben Jonson and John Heminges from London joined us. Mother set out a gorgeous feast of roast mutton, onions stewed with rosemary, and beef tongue thick with sauce. Canary wine flowed like nectar and honey in the house of Israel.

Jonson himself is a play writer like Father, and almost as popular. He's a bit on the heavy side, with quite formal manners, at least upon first meeting. He did warm up a bit when he and Father talked about the talents of Richard Burbage, the leading player in Father's troupe.

"One day, Will," said Jonson, "one of us must pen a play that will bring that man not just receipts at the theater, but a name that will be written forever on the wings of the muses that watch over our stages." Father smiled, and raised his glass in honor of Jonson's pledge.

Father told us the wonderful news that his company had signed a new lease on land across the river, lasting thirty-one years. They are to have their own theater! Father's days of sharing the stage with drooling bears are over. How anyone could think that tying a bear to a stake and watching him fend off a pack of dogs is entertainment is a mystery to me. Rawboned garlic eaters!

My father is now not only a member of the acting company but also a house sharer: part owner of a theater, as well as a sharer in the proceeds gained from the crowds who pay for an afternoon's entertainment. Some pretty opportunities there, I gather. Crafty calf's head! Father was willing to give all that up to save Edmund!

The new theater is to be called the Globe. Father marveled at all the improvements the carpenters will be adding as they finish construction. High galleries, carved balustrades, trap-doors, new tiring-houses, a deeply thatched roof, storage for all those pig bladders bursting with blood, a back balcony for cannon fire, and a front balcony for ghosts. The Globe will have it all. And with Father's plays acted within its walls, there will be no comparison in all of England.

Stratford, August 13, 1597. This evening I received communion from Father Wheeler. Afterward, Grandfather and I read over our spiritual last will and testament. I believe every word, so help me God.

Father returned to London today. I prayed that the angels guide him safely home again—and soon.

Stratford, August 15, 1597. I really enjoy having my own secret room. On its high walls I have hung sheaves of dried herbs to keep the smell of mother's cooking away. Lavender, basil, red mint, and chamomile are my personal favorites. Even with the plaster, open beams, and cobwebs, I like it here. But I don't dare store any sweet cakes or marzipan snacks in this room. The mice would be here in battalions and leave me not a single scrap.

Stratford, August 16, 1597. I received a letter from John today! He kept his promise! He tells me he will visit Swan Town on the nineteenth and will pay his respects to me and my family on that very morning! Trolls alive! I must prepare Mother and everyone else!

"This is the young man I've told you about, the one who saved my life in London," I explained to Mother excitedly.

"I am right glad that's he's coming to see you," she said. "But go slowly, Susanna. Although you're of courting age, remember to sift the wheat carefully, for there's many a harvest that's fallen short of its promise in this world, and a bitter harvest that can be."

Courting age? Zounds! Do I want this so soon? Although John's blue eyes do make my heart flutter, I don't yet know him very well.

Stratford, August 18, 1597. I have been working hard to get our house clean and swept for John's visit. There's still quite a bit of mess left from our moving in. Killed sixty-one fleas. And borrowed Peter Newman's gray cat, a real mouse killer. He dragged down four fat-bellied ones this morning.

Stratford, August 19, 1597. John knocked on our door before noon today! As my grandparents were due to visit for dinner, I thought it might be a good idea if John and I first took a short walk around town, with Mother and Judith to accompany us—at a distance, of course. It was so good to see him again! He looks very much the same, though his whiskers are a little thicker on his chin.

As we walked by the Clopton Bridge, Mother kept a sharp eye on us from nearby as she pretended to feed the swans with Judith. John told me he is staying with an old family friend of his on the edge of Swan Town. He revealed that he had thought often of our brief but exciting first meeting in London, amid all that smoke and falling books, and Edmund's miraculous release from prison. I admitted much the same, without adding that it was hard to believe that he had come all the way from Cambridge just to see me again.

"But I came here not just for a visit," said John. "I came here . . . I have come here for another very important reason, you see. What I really have come here for was to ask you if you would accept my offer of courtship—if your father approves, naturally."

"Well, my father is back in London," I said, "so that's not possible, at least today. But yes, I would be delighted if you would ask my grandfather, who could approve in my father's place, temporarily at least. When we go back, you can ask him. I would like that very much."

Amazingly, I said these words in a calm and even voice, even though my heart was beating away like a crazed drum about to burst. Thank God, the right words had come to me, after all. So far, at least. I had thought much about this moment, after Mother's comment the other day. I'd finally decided that young as I was, I liked John a great deal, and what better way to get to know him than during our courtship?

"Are you certain he'll approve?"

"Oh, I am very sure of Grandfather. He may joke a bit, but he'd never stand in our way, I just know it. And I am fairly certain my father will be the same. You saw how much both of them liked you in London. You could hardly do wrong, not after saving me from that deranged bookseller."

"I guess not," said John with a broad smile.

We moved out of the way of a noisy cart being pulled by

an old horse, its bony shoulders straining at the weight. It was still early, so traffic leaving or coming into town was light. When we reached the second arch of Clopton Bridge, we looked down into the swirling river.

"Look at the current below us," I said. "See how it flows out from under the bridge and then snaps back?"

"Why yes! That's quite a mystery. How did you discover this?"

"My father has taken us here ever since we could first walk. He'd show us the swiftly flowing current, and then point out this great mystery of our dear River Avon."

"It must be due to some strange rock formation directly under the bridge."

"Father used to tell us the river's current was time's flowing course and only here was it called back, repeatedly rescued by a miracle of love, for that's the only thing in this world that can transcend time's rushing course. Something like that."

"Yes, something like that," said John, glancing at me with a smile.

My eye caught Mother sixty paces or so away, watching us serenely and very carefully. I hoped she was thinking, *Here is the prospect of a good harvest*. A harvest rooted in the heart, I believe.

"Of course, others say the town council drowned a witch here," I said, "but that was before I was born. Nowadays, it seems they only punish harmless women on this bridge. I like Father's story much better."

Later. When we returned to New Place, my chest felt light and fluttery, as if it were made of feathers or butterfly wings. The uncles were out fishing on the river and weren't joining us. Thank God! I didn't need them to play some kind of comic chorus to this important scene in my life. Though I was confident of Grandfather's approval, this was all very new to me.

"Good day to you both," said John, bowing and taking off his cap as Grandmother and Grandfather walked into the parlor by the big fireplace. Mother had set out tankards of cider and ale. I noticed for the first time that John's boots and jacket were new.

Grandmother was taking him in from head to foot, and Grandfather seemed only mildly happy to see him again. Perhaps he was thinking of John's remarks about his Puritanism.

"And how might you be, young Hall?" asked Grandfather. "Still dodging pistols, are ye?"

"Not since that last encounter in London, thankfully," responded John.

"Well, that's a cause for celebration, I gather. But come," added Grandfather, "join me in front of this fire, and tell me what brings you to Stratford."

"I really came to see Susanna," answered John, "and all of you, of course."

"It's not every day I get to see a man who has saved my life," I said while looking at Mother, who was busy stirring some pots hanging over the fire. When the time came for Father's approval of John's courtship, I knew I had to have my mother on my side. But one thing at a time, I said to myself.

"What a wonderful house you have here," John said. "I'd love to be able to buy a place like this someday, though I'm sure I would have to work hard for it."

"What sort of work are you interested in?" asked Grandmother.

"I study medicine at Cambridge. It's really all I've ever wanted to do in my life."

"Let me see your hands," Grandfather demanded suddenly.

"Grandfather, John's our guest, not a worker in your glovery," I said, embarrassed.

"It's no trouble," said John, putting out his hands. Grandfather grabbed them both and held then tightly in his own, then turned John's palms upward and looked at them closely. Finally, he let them go.

"You've right strong hands for someone who's still at university."

"Usually I return home every three weeks or so and help my father out, cut him some wood, tend to his garden, that sort of thing. Nothing very difficult, though it's saved me from having hands too soft for hard work."

"A doctor without strong hands is a useless railing knave—that you'll see, boy. Keep those hands strong for work and you'll heal bodies and hearts enough, I can tell you that."

"No doubt, sir," said John.

Grandfather then wasted no time getting to his biggest concern. "And your faith, son," he said.

"Yes, what of it, sir?"

"You told us in London that because of your Puritan leanings, you've not ever visited a playhouse before. But you'd court a playwright's daughter? How is that?" asked Grandfather, his eyes questioning.

"While my faith forbids me to approve of the many sinful

things that take place around the playhouses you speak of, sir, I know the difference between the plow that furrows and the worm that turns, if you catch my meaning, sir."

"I do, though I hope my granddaughter understands you too," said Grandfather. "There is no reason to tiptoe around the real reason for your visit, young man. Courtships must begin on common ground, or they'll come to no good, no good at all."

"Of course I understand," I said. "Poets such as Father can't be blamed for the rabble that sometimes crowds their stages."

"True enough," answered Grandfather with a smile.

"How old are you?" Judith piped up.

"Judith!" I yelled.

"That's no trouble either. If you must know, I turned twenty-one years old a few months ago, and I'm not too young to start courting the prettiest young woman in Stratford, with your permission."

Judith rolled her eyes as if she had bitten into a sour apple. No one said anything for a moment.

Amid the silence, a rumbling sound began to come from Grandfather's direction. His belly began to jiggle. Then he started wheezing with his great roaring laugh that could split the very air with its joy. He finally said: "Well, that's a brave boy in love if I ever saw one in my life. Of course you have my permission, lad. I just wonder why Susanna didn't run off with you in the first place!"

Stratford, August 21, 1597. The weather is hot, and Swan Town's streets stink of horse droppings and other muck. Thank God we keep our house and yard reasonably neat! In the late afternoon, John came over for supper and met uncles Richard and Gilbert. It wasn't very long before they teased him a little, and joked about his whiskers and his Puritanism. Thank heavens that brand of religion has not influenced John too strongly. He seems only to be sincerely pious.

Stratford, August 22, 1597. While I was walking home from market today with Judith and mother, John surprised us. In front of everyone he gave me a bouquet of country flowers, wet with morning dew.

I didn't blush. Not much, anyway.

Stratford, August 30, 1597. Toad-spotted churl! Father arrived from London last night and utterly disapproves of my courtship with John. Because John Hall is a Puritan, Father *forbids* any further contact. Though he is grateful for John's help in London, he says he's not obligated to give his daughter away to every lucky jack, especially a Puritan one! Thankfully John is visiting some sick folk in nearby Snitterfield for a few days, and wasn't here for the awful scene.

Father's demands are so wrong, so utterly unreasonable, they seem to have sprung from some nightmare region of Hell instead of my very own father. Unbounded tyrant! There he sat with Grandfather by the kitchen fire cracking nuts and drinking ale, the matter settled.

"I don't understand! John saved my life in London. And Edmund's, for that matter. How could you be so ungrateful as to refuse to let him court me after all that?"

"Precisely because I realize the value of what he has saved, my love. Besides, if you'll remember, religious controversy is what got Edmund into trouble in the first place. And nearly got you shot."

Grandfather looked at Father and mumbled something about joining Grandmother and Mother out in the back garden. Dear Grandfather! Though I knew he sympathized with me, I also knew he would never contradict my father's authority in such a matter.

A moment went by before either of us spoke. The fire crackled before us, its flames warming several blackened pots Mother had set simmering for supper.

"And I am just supposed to forget about John, act as if nothing happened in St. Paul's that day, act as if I haven't a heart at all? Act as if he were a Montague and I some forlorn Capulet. Is that it?"

Father let my question linger in the air a moment. I could tell I had made my point by referring to one of his very own stories of forbidden, tragic love.

"Susanna, that's for the stage, not everyday living," responded Father calmly. "You know better than that."

"Do I?"

"You do. The divisions that pull this island apart on religious grounds strike at our family on many fronts. The dangers of practicing the old pieties are well known to you now. As are the daggers pointing toward our playhouses in London. If I let John Hall court you, I might bring such divisions right into the heart of this family, and that I'm not willing to do. It's too risky, and besides, he's just one boy; there are many others for you. You're bright enough, and pretty enough too," he added in a softened tone, thinking that now he had made his point.

"I thought you said we should judge a man by what he

does, not by what faith he professes."

"I did say that, and I believe it still. But someone's faith, these days, also matters a great deal. The crown has seen to that, I'm afraid. You must see that I do this only for your safety."

He reached out for my hand. I pulled away and stonily addressed the fire more than him, my heart in tatters.

"You are my father, and I will obey you. But I have never felt more alone, or more betrayed, in my life."

"Susanna, no, listen to me, please," said Father, his eyes shining with tears. But it was no good, for I myself had begun to cry and simply had to leave, had to be alone.

"I love you, but I cannot abide the horrid refusal you have dropped on my head today."

I fled up to my room and with great effort restrained an impulse to slam the door. O treason of the blood! I hate the word—and the world—that would keep John Hall out of my life. How could Father be so blind?

Stratford, August 31, 1597. I feel like I am in a prison, bound by rules and laws I did not make and do not understand. All around me—here in Swan Town, and in London—I see the savagery of Her Majesty's laws against old believers. Chapels defaced, an innocent woman drowned, whole families punished horribly, and my own uncle almost quartered like an animal for merely putting his hand to an old ratty play. What a kingdom of fools!

And now, in my own family, more harsh misrule, more attempts to control my life, not even taking into account what I feel. John Hall has behaved honorably to me, has even saved my life. He professes no irrational zeal like other Puritans, only a mild leaning to their purer doctrines. And what does my father do? He flatly refuses to let John court me!

I realize I promised Judith I'd stop working on *The Parrot King*, at least for a little while. Well, although that was only weeks ago, much has changed since then. I know now that writing plays like Father is the only way I can use the wits that I've been given in life. I even think this idea is already worked into my script. For when I satirize Her Majesty's realm as nothing but an island-size cage full of mindless parrots echoing words that will make them safe, but definitely not free, I am also sadly describing my own home, my very own father. And I refuse to parrot words that are not mine, words that strike against my heart with their harsh denials and refusals.

Stratford, September 1, 1597. Father married Mother when he was barely eighteen. He should know how I feel. He will know how angry I am after I finish my play and it sends the Swan into roars of laughter and delight.

Stratford, September 2, 1597. More confusion. I am drowning in it. Grandfather and I had a long talk today. He said that Sir Colin Hill is stepping up his investigations into rumors that people are harboring priests in their homes and spreading old catechisms about. We need to be more cautious than ever about practicing the old faith now, and that includes our dealings with those who belong to another church. I know Grandfather told me this to try to make Father's refusal easier to bear, to blame it on the times we live in instead of on Father's stubbornness. I wish I could see it this way, but I simply can't. That is why I am writing this entry so late, and why

I will finish my play only in the small hours of the night, when barely a soul is awake.

Grandfather also said I still have some years before accepting a gentleman's hand anyway. When I awoke, three fleas had bitten my left arm. Three stars, just like Orion's belt. Pish! Or Cupid's silly arrows.

Tomorrow, Judith and I are going to visit Maggie the Mystic. She's a widow on the edge of town who, it is said, can see what to us is nothing but darkness. The future, I mean.

Stratford, September 3, 1597. My visit to Maggie the Mystic has not done much to inspire my belief in self-appointed prophets. Even though her house was a little frightening—with all those shadows, at least seven cats slinking about, and more lit candles than I've ever seen—I just don't believe that she speaks "for the Spirit of our terrible God," as she says. I don't think God is terrible. St. John says He is love. And I certainly don't believe that Maggie's "mystic wound" flows with the blood of Christ. Smelled more like chicken blood to me.

And what should I make of her prophecy: "The son will save the father; a brother for a new son." I'd bet a bushel of hazelnuts that there's more commerce than mysticism going on at Maggie's house.

Stratford, September 4, 1597. What happened to the father who used to make me laugh so? Where has he gone?

Stratford, September 5, 1597. This morning I went up to my secret room above the kitchen to read and think in privacy.

I had read through part of my prayers when I heard Father's voice in the kitchen. He and Mother were alone. It was market day, I remembered, and they probably thought I was in town with the rest of the family. Yet here I am, in the darkness of my room, feet against the warm stones of the chimney flue, and what do I overhear? Mother and Father talking about John. About me!

"Do you think she'll be ready for him then?" Father asked.

"I do . . . just give her a few years, two or three, and then she'll know."

Know what?

"And you think he'll really tolerate her belief in the old faith? Can she trust him? Can *we* trust him?"

"If he loves her," Mother said, "he'll come back when he's done studying and renew his courtship. He seems like a right fine man, he does, and a keeper of his word."

"I suppose so, except for that Puritanism of his. Yet he seems more devout than angry, as so many of those black-hearted theater haters are."

"Will, he's said nought a word against the theaters since I've laid eyes on him."

"I know it—that's why I think he'd make a good husband. In two or three years. When Susanna's ready too."

Mother must have been preparing dinner—the sound of her knife on the table board was strong and sure. It was a sound we all knew well: Mother's mind was made up. My heart filled with hope. Had she swayed Father?

"Just keep it between us for a little while. If he's meant for her . . . well, he'll be back, is all," said Mother.

"Like all those May mornings we had together. What

promises we made, out on your father's meadows," said Father.

"You're here, aren't you?" Mother said with a laugh.

Tardy-gaited fortune! How lucky an eavesdropper I have become! But now the difficult part. I have to pretend I know nothing of my father's decision to let John resume his courtship when he has finished his studies. If I told them I knew, it might influence them for the worse, or put new restrictions on where I can go or what I can do in the future. God's lid! That's all I'd need.

I waited a short while before venturing below.

"Why, Susanna, I didn't know you were home," said Mother when I came down the stairs into the kitchen.

"I was going to go with Judith and the uncles," I answered, "but I fell asleep while reading instead." I had messed my hair up before coming down, and yawned before I spoke for good effect.

"We were just talking about you," said Father, "and are hoping you will take my decision that John Hall is not the man for you with the obedience proper to a young girl of your intelligence. It's for your own good that we do this. A man from another faith—in these times anyway—is no man to marry. I am sorry, but my decision is final, for you must understand—"

"I do, Father."

"—that we have close ties to many of the old faith in this town, and elsewhere, and even a Puritan can be dangerous when he's—"

"Yes, I understand."

"You what?" said Father, confused at my sudden conversion. Had I given in too easily?

"She said she *understands*, Will . . . she's agreeing with you," chimed in Mother, saving my hasty capitulation from disaster.

I picked up the skimmer in the fireplace and pushed the ashes to the corner. Perhaps some cooking would be in order. Something to show them I had accepted Father's decision with a good heart. Which I have, of course! Little does he know!

"Susanna, I should have known you'd come around," said Father. "You are mature enough to understand. Some other young men from town will come to court you, you'll see."

I felt the sudden desire to blacken every young man in Swan Town with some choice adjectives, but forced myself to refrain.

I smiled instead.

Stratford, September 7, 1597. Of course, while this domestic drama was going on at New Place, John was away in Snitterfield and had no idea that our courtship was threatened with a shorter life than a spring rose with a worm in its heart. With Judith's help, I have now managed to meet with him and tell him everything. Though at first shocked, he was very pleased that my father had privately changed his mind about our courtship.

At this point, I also thought it time to tell John the truth about my family's connections to the ancient beliefs now persecuted by the crown. I knew it was a risk, but I also knew in my heart that I can trust him.

"You see, Susanna," he said, after I explained my family's secret, "that's what the past fifty years and more have done to the faith in this country. Families and whole towns and cities pray in fear of the state, of spies for the crown. My faith tells me something different about God and His church than the faith of your family does, but the truly important thing is for all of us to follow our consciences. Your father isn't to blame for disapproving of our courting; he is only doing what he thinks is right."

"How could it be right when it separates us?"

"It won't for long, as you yourself heard him say. Thank the Lord he's come around and at least eventually will let me court you," he said, putting his arm around me. "It will take two years at most for me to finish my studies. You may not hear from me for months at a time. But I will come to visit you here in Stratford—when your father's away in London, of course."

Sharing this secret with John has brought us closer than ever before.

Stratford, September 8, 1597. John took leave today for Cambridge, though he says he will visit as soon as possible. Beneath my sadness at his leaving lies the joy of knowing he loves me and Father will one day approve our courtship. Until then, I must act like a good daughter, obedient to her father's will. Also, it's exciting to have a secret romance.

I have decided that over the coming months I shall not pine away for John as lovers in stories and fables do. For one thing, an outright rebellion against Father might endanger his secret decision. But if I seem obedient, Father most likely will attribute it to my maturity, and may give in sooner. So it's not the time for cowardly fits of fainting. For now I intend to leave few corners of Swan Town unexplored. Even if I have to drag

Judith with me every step of the way!

And then, of course, there is my play. I plan to finish it, even if it doesn't see the light of day on Father's stage. There's something very satisfying about turning one's anger and irritation into a disciplined line of language, even if it is rather humble, like my play. I suppose if there were no restrictions on my life, I might not write such a satire. Since it seems that day is not coming anytime soon, there is plenty of work for my quill to do. And who knows—if I finish *The Parrot King*, and see it performed somewhere, Father may decide that I am not the girl-child he thinks I am. Zounds! Courtship could come sooner than I think!

Stratford, September 9, 1597. I am practicing not smiling. It isn't as easy as I thought. There's a sunrise in my heart, but I can't let on. I will accept my father's will with patience.

Especially knowing he agrees with me.

Stratford, September 10, 1597. Mother is very pleased I am taking Father's decision as well as I am. She says I am growing up in mind as well as body. 'Tis true! I have taken to acting and playing the roles that make for peace. Players, as Father well knows, are survivors, if nothing else.

Stratford, September 11, 1597. Father left today for London. He is pleased at my obedience. So am I!

Stratford, September 21, 1597. Today John visited for a whole afternoon! It was so wonderful to see him again. Judith again acted as messenger after John tugged her sleeve at the marketplace shortly before noon. She told me to go to the north side of the market square in one hour. Luckily, Mother was distracted with some work in the orchard, so I slipped out.

He looked so handsome standing in the sun, waiting for me. He nodded politely and then gestured for me to follow him down the riverside, past the town square, to where we could walk unnoticed by the gossipy women of Swan Town.

John told me of his studies, his long hours poring over musty books and examining bodies stolen from city graves in the dead of night. He wonders at the marvels of the human frame, and the mysteries of herbs and their healing powers on mind and body. I reminded John how exciting I found London compared to Swan Town, and how I hoped we didn't have to wait for another crazed bookseller to bring us together again.

"Think of the miraculous reversal in the Avon's current you showed me," said John as we walked through knee-high grass down the river from the market. "We will return to each other, let time do what it may."

"I trust you," I answered. "How could I do otherwise?"

He gave my hand a warm squeeze, and we continued on for a little while before he rode back to Cambridge and his books.

I am tired. After I got home, I had to do three times the work in the kitchen so Mother wouldn't notice any unfinished tasks. My fingers smell of lavender, thyme, and sage. They shall weave dreams tonight.

Stratford, September 24, 1597. I am up to my eyebrows drying herbs from our garden. Lemon thyme, tarragon, chamomile, foxglove, cowslips, tansy, henbane, monkshood, and mint fill our house with their powerful fragrance.

Stratford, September 25, 1597. I received a note today from John delivered by one of Mother's friends. His studies are going well. He says he'll try to visit sometime soon. So I pray!

Stratford, September 26, 1597. Today I took up my play again. Because I decided it is to be a prologue, it must be short. So far I have polished like silver the opening speech (a part I was born for, I think), and sketched out the rest, in which I show how the foolish laws of the parrot kingdom (cleverly disguised, of course) are like a dreaded, dissembling chaff-brain who deserves a public knock on the pate. The groundlings should love it!

Four

" … bones that rattle in the wind … "

Stratford, September 30, 1597. After finishing my work, I spent much of this afternoon sitting beneath a lime tree near Hamnet's grave. Leaves spun around me in the breeze. Each one seemed a question, drifting as it would on time's steady stream. Will John and I really court someday? Will my play ever be anything more than the silly scribbling of a girl banished from the magical world of the theater? Whatever befalls me, I now know nothing good happens in this world of ours without a brave backbone and a crafty quill!

Stratford, October 3, 1597. Despite rainy weather, John arrived this morning with Adam, a boy about twelve who is his newly hired assistant. John's training as a physician now has him assigned to treating patients on a part-time basis, so he has wisely chosen Swan Town and its surrounding villages to complete this round of his schooling. Adam is the son of a widow who lives in a town north of here. John says he is quite clever and wants to become a doctor someday. He's clearly a great help as John treats in small and sundry ways some of our local folk who have come down with various illnesses.

I had Judith cover for me by saying that I was helping the widow Henley with her kitchen and such and would be back in a few hours. Although I don't like telling such little untruths, knowing that my parents secretly approve of John makes me believe that it's not so bad to hold back on expressing one's true feelings or hiding one's intentions every now and then. Grandfather once told me that Her Majesty herself said at the beginning of her reign that she had no intention of looking into men's souls when she governed. God's lid! Would she had been true to such wisdom!

After introducing me to Adam, John sent him off to fish along the river. John and I went to the Bear Tavern, and amid the back tables, out of eyeshot of anyone I knew, we talked for hours. John said he might not be able to visit for some time, as he had new examinations to study for at Cambridge, but after that, well . . . it won't be long before he'll be known as Dr. Hall, and so will need to choose a town in which to settle. I suggested a place I know as Swan Town. Although at times too quiet, it has been known to raise beautiful women of the marrying kind. How John did laugh!

Of course, I mentioned nothing about my play. Even Judith doesn't know I've been working on it again. I did tell John how Grandfather wasn't feeling well, and he gave me a few medicinal herbs we haven't tried yet. One contained oil of violets and smelled of spring, I swear. Our good-bye was bittersweet. This role of pretending not to be in love is getting wearisome.

Stratford, October 4, 1597. Grandfather has taken to some of John's medicine. The oil of violets especially. When he asked me where I got them, I had to make something up about a new booth at market. Grandfather looked suspicious for a moment but said nothing.

Stratford, October 5, 1597. Several people in Swan Town have been arrested. Charges include treason and harboring of priests. Sir Colin Hill and his brutish crew must be on the prowl.

Stratford, October 6, 1597. The rumors have proven to be true. Sir Colin Hill is on the move again. With the council's approval, he has begun to sweep through the town.

Mother is worried. Philip Rogers, the apothecary on High Street, has asked us to hide his son Arthur, who is preparing to go off to Douai, a city in France, to study for the priesthood. The secret route out of the country and across the Channel must be prepared in advance, so Arthur would have to stay with us for a week or two. Mr. Rogers has offered to help fix up one of the secret rooms in our house for the purpose of hiding Arthur. He says Sir Colin went through his own house last week by candlelight and examined every nook and cranny. Even charged him two shillings for the candles.

I don't know what to think. If we are caught hiding suspected Catholics, we may lose everything. Yet not to help? Impossible.

Stratford, October 7, 1597. After a long night in prayer, we have agreed to help Mr. Rogers. Tonight he is coming over to help prepare a hiding place for his son. If we have to turn our home into a modern-day catacomb, so be it.

Stratford, October 8, 1597. Last night I could hear Sir Colin's horse trot down our street. *Clip. Clop. Clip. Clop.* As he passed, we snuffed out our candles and waited in the darkness. Uncle Gilbert stood watch at a top-floor window. When he gave the signal, we resumed work. Grandfather has secured shelves in front of the hideaway next to the fireplace in the second-floor guest room. With planking, plaster, and specially sized hinges, we're confident that no one will be able to detect anything. A side entrance from Father's study provides a way for Mother to get food and water in. Being so close to the fireplace, it should be right snug, and—

(I must go, Uncle Gilbert whistles). Darkness, hide us now.

Stratford, October 9, 1597. The secret room is ready. Tonight Arthur Rogers comes in from Coughton Court, northwest of here. The air is cold and foggy. I might have to neglect my journal while Arthur is with us. I dare not provide any cause for visitation from Sir Colin. I want to go to my secret room and wait and wait and then come out when another century has rolled around. God and his angels be with us. Amen.

Stratford, October 19, 1597. Our special visitor left us tonight. He makes for Dover by darkness, and thence to Douai for his studies. The last few days were a near thing. I thought for certain Sir Colin had found us out. Two days ago he started visiting several houses on Chapel Street with warrants signed by the town bailiff. When Sir Colin's knock came on our door shortly after supper yesterday, there was little we could do but hope the old man wouldn't rip our walls apart.

Mother was tight-lipped, tense. Grandfather sat by the fire, a welcome visitor in Father's absence. Judith offered Sir Colin some cider (*As hot and scalding as the brimstone you threaten us with, sir!*). He seemed to be rummaging about his teeth with his tongue, searching for remnants of his supper. The jowls on either side of his face sagged like bags of flour flung over a horse's back.

His hard eyes raked over us in the uneasy silence.

I met his glare but said nothing.

"Word is, Mrs. Shakespeare, that there's a Jesuit student hiding in this town. Waiting for a chance to spread his heresies, laying schemes for the overthrow of our lawful government. Now, you know right well that hiding such a man is contrary to the wishes of Her Majesty's council, that such crimes are liable to the severest sanctions imaginable. They are treasonous without doubt."

Mother's face lost all color. Goats and monkeys! I felt my knees start to shake, and held on to them as if they were pigeons about to fly off.

"You see I've come here alone," continued Sir Colin. "I simply want to find out what you know about this, is all."

"We know nothing," Mother said.

"The woman's right, Sir Colin," Grandfather said. "We know nothing but our own business, which I assure you is not treason. But have a look around, see for yourself. We've nothing to hide."

"John!"

"Anne, let the man see for himself," Grandfather said.

Sir Colin walked past us and into the back rooms. My journal was hidden in my desk only a few feet from his face, but he turned and climbed the stairs.

From upstairs came heavy noises, as if furniture were being moved, doors opened and shut, walls checked for hidden passageways. Poor Arthur! Surely his time—and ours—had come.

"Angels and ministers of grace, defend us," prayed Mother in a whisper.

More time passed. No shouts, no struggles. Silence.

Then Sir Colin reappeared in our main room, his eyes still looking around, as if he were unwilling to give up without an arrest.

"Mrs. Shakespeare, I am sorry to disturb you like this. Everything appears to be as it should," said Sir Colin, his face showing severe disappointment, almost as if he had missed a really splendid feast.

"As I expected. Good night, sir," Mother replied.

We sat, breathless and still, for a few moments. Finally, we could wait no longer and ran upstairs to our hidden guest. As I walked into the room, I saw the secret panel slowly opening, with Arthur on the short bed we had built into the passage.

By candlelight, his face was as angelic as that of a child of five.

Stratford, October 25, 1597. It's been almost a week since Arthur left us for the Continent. Philip Rogers was most grateful to us for keeping his son safe. He'd do it for one of ours, Mother told him. And Arthur is a fine, brave man. For ten days and nights, he stayed hidden. When the sun set, Mother would bring him some food and drink and let him walk around the main room for a few hours. Taking turns, we spent time talking to him. Though a scholar, he has no airs about him. He even tried to reteach Uncle Richard some of the Latin he'd forgotten since school.

Stratford, October 26, 1597. While Judith and I were at our tasks in the kitchen today, I decided to ask Mother more about Sir Colin Hill.

"What makes him hate followers of the old faith?" I wondered while I worked at my spinning wheel in a corner of the kitchen. "I don't understand how someone could be so intent on putting people in the stocks, or worse, for what they believe."

"Or worse is right," replied Mother as she finished plucking a chicken for our dinner. "Sir Colin has sent many in these parts to complete financial ruin, and those are the lucky ones, I can tell you."

Judith was cutting herbs for the stew and was surrounded by mounds of thyme, marjoram, and rosemary. She seemed to take delight in chopping with a particularly vicious stroke whenever Sir Colin's name was mentioned.

"Sir Colin is crafty, and you'll do well to avoid his eye," said Mother as she placed the quartered chicken into a steaming pot, "and you must continue to go with us now and then to Trinity so you don't raise suspicion. Remember never to make the sign of the cross in public, for that would be like putting your own neck in a noose, it would."

"Grandfather's told me all this before," I said.

"And good advice it is, Susanna," answered Mother.

"But why does Sir Colin work with such a vengeance?" asked Judith. "What have we ever done to him?"

"Not us, but his very own brother," Mother said. "That's the reason Sir Colin burns with such hatred, if you ask me. Before you were born, he used to be a glover, just like your grandfather. Then he got knighted—his wife comes from good stock—and Sir Colin thought the world owed him everything. But when his younger brother decided to leave for France and become a Jesuit, why, he nearly lost his mind. He took title to his brother's property based on what he saw as his act of treason against the queen by following the old faith."

"That's an awful man," said Judith.

"That's not the end of it either," said Mother. "His brother returned some years later to London and was caught, arrested, and hanged on Tyburn Hill, a martyr. Some say Sir Colin turned in his own brother for the reward money and to make sure he would never lose his brother's land. Others say that the soul of his executed brother haunts him still, and that's why Sir Colin roams about, restlessly hunting down as many of the old faith as he can find. He piles his coffers with money, hoping with his ill-gotten gains to silence the voice of his conscience."

"And perhaps of the spirit of his betrayed brother?" I asked.

"True enough, Susanna," said Mother. "Sir Colin is a man driven by ghosts and gold, and for that reason doubly dangerous."

Stratford, October 27, 1597. Mother received a letter today from Father. The theater is busier than ever. He had some sad news, however. Nathan Miller, one of Father's players, has died of plague. How terrible! Father and his players paid for the funeral services, and had the great bell rung for an hour for his soul. How quickly one may drink an ale one day, amid laughter and friends, and the next be fitted for a winding sheet and a player's grave.

I shall pray for Nathan Miller.

Stratford, October 28, 1597. Uncle Gilbert asked Judith and me to help him clean Grandfather's shop this afternoon. Grandfather and Richard had gone on a short trip to buy some deer and goat hides, and so Gilbert had to handle the shop on his own.

A pox on the shop! I have never seen such a tangle of knives, scrapers, hammers, nails, tongs, awls, vises, hooks, and ropes in all my life! How do they make sense of any of this?

"You get used to it after a while," said Gilbert, pushing his long but thinning hair out his eyes, "and it's some satisfaction, let me tell you, to see coming out of this chaos of hides and blades a lady's smooth calfskin glove, or a right handsome saddle fit for an earl."

I suppose my journal does much the same for me. Out of the confusion of my days comes a page I have written myself and arranged as I see fit, not as others would dictate or demand.

Stratford, October 29, 1597. I saw a man today who looked so much like John from behind and far away that when I saw him, my heart fluttered faster than a finch's wing.

Stratford, October 30, 1597. Uncle Richard carved a fine walking stick for Grandfather this week. Grandfather's been having a bit of trouble with his balance, and this should help. It's of solid oak, with an eagle's head at the top, the eyes and beak stern and imposing. "I'll take it with me on my daily walks across town and over Clopton Bridge," Grandfather said. I like to sit by the bank with him, watching the fields sway in the autumn breezes. I think almost every swan on the river will feed from my hand by now.

Stratford, November 1, 1597. Father and Edmund arrived from London today. Father had some local business to attend to, and was glad to slip away from the theater for a few days. Edmund is now a full member of the Chamberlain's Men, and Father says he's doing wonderfully well. He gets his lines well enough, and is popular with the regulars at the theater.

"The Swan is one of the premier theaters in the kingdom, of that there's no doubt. And your father is setting more records for attendance than anyone in London. Aren't you, Will?" said Edmund.

"The company is doing right well," answered Father.

"Don't listen to his modesty, Susanna, for your father's name on a play will guarantee a huge audience every afternoon for a year straight," crowed Edmund. O my dear uncle, how you read my mind! My father's name on my prologue is just the key I need to get it staged. Now all that remains is to finish my play—and get to the Swan.

Stratford, November 2, 1597. Today the sky cleared at sunset, huge streaks of purple clouds peeling off the horizon as the sun slipped down into darkness. A full moon sat low in the sky.

"Let's take a walk," said Father, after an hour or so of sitting by the fire. "The wind's whipping strong and it's such a clear night. Come on!"

"I'll go," I said, getting my cloak from a peg near the fireplace.

No one else wanted to join us, so Father and I made our way down Henley Street toward Trinity Church. The rain had indeed left us, though the streets still shone under the moonlight. Smells of wet hay, horses, rotting leaves, and discarded vegetables filled the air. A dog barked at nothing in particular.

We walked past house after house, some shuttered, some not; past the Henley Street house, its top right-hand window lit by a single slender candle ("Grandfather must be up, sitting by the fire"); past the Guild Chapel, draped in silence. Wind whipped up and down the empty streets.

The squat and solid tower of the church rose up past the lane of lime trees leading to its entrance. The moon shed a ghostly light. Shadows sheared off in long lines and sharply angled shapes.

"Here lie Stratford's departed sons and daughters. They sleep sheltered from the storms of life, until the last trumpet shatters the great frame of the world," said Father as we walked toward the church. "I want to be buried here," he continued. "Inside the church, of course."

I looked at him, rather surprised to hear him speak so calmly about his own death, but said nothing. We walked in silence around the front of the church, past the leaning rows of gravestones, sentinels of sorrow and remembrance.

Before long, we stood before Hamnet's gravestone. Father dropped to his knees and began to pray. I joined him, for the memories of my brother came almost as quickly as the tears I wiped away from my eyes. The short life of our little Puck rose up before us, radiant even in the shadow of eternity.

After a few moments, we stood and looked across the dark graveyard. My throat felt tight, my voice the thinnest of reeds.

"I miss him still," I said.

"As is right, my dear," replied Father. "You know, in my mind's eye I have come here every night since that terrible day when Hamnet was taken from us. For a time, even as I realized how often the plague strikes down the young especially, I just couldn't accept it. And I felt Heaven was deaf to my grief. But over the months, a peace has come to me. Every loss in this life, I now know, is not merely a loss, but also a tug into that other world where gravestones are unknown, and where little boys don't sicken and die in an afternoon. But believe me, if there were any other way to such wisdom, I would walk through fire to gain it."

"I'm surprised you could still write your plays after losing Hamnet," I said.

"I chose to write other tales, full of clowning and magic. Some things take a little time before they can rise to the surface in ink. I've started a play about a legendary Dane known as Hamlet, a prince of Denmark. He's a right clever one, just like our Hamnet. It just might be my greatest work when I finish it, and its mystery will be one with the joy and the sorrow that Hamnet's life has brought to us, I can tell you that."

I held Father's hand for a moment, grateful that he had shared with me thoughts so close to his heart.

"Look, the charnel house," he said suddenly. "Let's see if it's open."

North of the churchyard, adjoining the chancel, stood a two-storied structure with a vicar's study on the top floor and a bone house beneath. When spaces in the churchyard grew scarce, and the freshly dead needed a resting place, a grave was dug up and the old bones were tossed into the charnel house. Stratford's graveyard being small, the pile of bones grew higher with each passing year. It had cost Father an extra ten shillings to insure that Hamnet's grave wouldn't suffer a similar fate.

"When I was a child, this was the scariest place in town. Gilbert and Richard and I used to dare each other to knock on its door at night," he said.

"I'm not sure it's any less frightening now."

"True enough . . . for in here is the greatest mystery," he replied. "I've always wanted to at least take a peek inside. Let's see."

The door was covered with moss and clinging ivy.

"Help me with this," he said.

We tugged at the handle. As it gave way, heavy rusted iron hinges squealed, then stopped with a high-pitched squawk. A sickly-sweet odor crept out of the place, lodging in our nostrils almost like the smell of incense swaying from a censer at mass.

"Want to go in?" asked Father.

"After you," I said with a nervous smile.

"Follow me."

Though we took only a step or two inside, we could see that the room was large. Several grated windows on one side threw an angle of moonlight across the floor. All manner of bones, heaped higher than a man, formed four huge piles, bleached of color, of sense, of life. Ribs, hips, femurs, skulls, jaws, tiny square bones belonging to hands or feet, littered the room.

Father gasped at the sight and held on to the open door for support. A gust of wind tried to blow the door shut. He steadied it, making sure it wouldn't close with us inside.

"Something is rotten in the town of Stratford, and I think we've found it," he said, with only a hint of jesting in his voice.

"I hope none of us are thrown in here, fool and wit pitched into the same smelly heap," I said, my voice echoing off the damp walls.

Father picked up a skull from the heap of bones and turned its hollow eyes upward.

"Are we no more than this?" I asked. "Bones that rattle in the wind?" I lightly touched the skull's brow.

"No one can answer that question for you," he replied, "at least not completely. For we see through a glass darkly."

In the cold air, I struggled to suppress a shiver that wanted to climb up one side of my body and down the other.

"We shouldn't be afraid of death, Susanna, though it may take years to learn how. At such sorrowful partings, life is changed, not ended."

Neither of us said anything for a moment or two. A gust of wind outside snapped across the churchyard, a lonely whisper.

"Aye, it must be so," I said, grabbing his hand. "But mercy! This place is damp and rheumy. . . . Let's go back."

And so we went out, shutting the door tightly behind us. We walked up to the steps of the church, where we sat for nearly an hour. The sky wheeled its thousands of stars above us, each turning in its splendor, links of light spilling out of endless black.

Stratford, November 3, 1597. Margaret Kempson, wife of the schoolmaster at our grammar school, brought me a letter from John today! Her husband, Robert, studied at Cambridge, and knew John's brother.

John has been studying for his degree every waking hour. So far, his work has met with high praise. On rare occasions, he visits London with some of his fellow students, and has even seen a play once or twice. He had better stay away from the Swan! Best of all, his work in and around Swan Town has led him to inquire about setting up a practice here, as he promised. I had to share his letter with Judith. It's simply too good to keep to myself.

Stratford, November 4, 1597. Grandfather is not well. He breathes heavily and is tired even after long naps. His eyes are yellowish and weak. "A noisy bunch with the best goods of any glover around." That's Grandfather, talking about how he'd like his family to be remembered. He talks as if death is very near.

Stratford, November 5, 1597. Grandfather let me read his spiritual testament today, expressing belief in the old faith. It's a sad day in this glorious kingdom when men such as he have to declare their faith secretly, before the angels of Heaven yet hidden from men who hold power without the least fear of God in their hearts. No wonder Grandfather has such papers secreted carefully inside the walls of his house. St. Michael keep them—and us—safe!

Stratford, November 7, 1597. Yesterday my grandfather died. I can write no more.

Stratford, November 9, 1597. I spent all day in my room, alone. Only in the late afternoon did I get out of my nightgown and dress and come downstairs. It's so funny the thoughts one gets sitting quiet. I saw from my window the tower of Trinity Church, flat and square against the sky. If we hide in our rooms, will death find us? Why isn't there something we could put over our doors like the Hebrews did to keep that dark angel away?

Stratford, November 12, 1597. Grandfather was laid to rest today in Trinity churchyard. Edmund and Father returned for the burial, many relatives came from the countryside, and of course many of Grandfather's friends were there. Late at night, we attended a funeral mass at Langton Farm, a few miles north of Swan Town. About twenty-five people in all were there. The priest's black robes seemed darker than night itself, the very color of sorrow. Seeing so many of Grandfather's friends joining us in this secret, forbidden ceremony added to my sense of how loved he was in life, and how blessed.

Father was quite downcast. He brightened after mass, though, describing Grandfather as the best and kindest man he ever knew, a man who loved with a heart as broad as the sky.

Judith and I prayed for Grandfather's soul before bed. Judith added a special prayer for Hamnet too. "I know we will meet Hamnet and Grandfather someday in Heaven," she said. "Hamnet will flash that silly smile of his, and Grandfather will chuckle as if the court of Heaven itself were his hearthstone." I could add nothing to this but a whispered "Amen."

Stratford, November 14, 1597. Father and Edmund left for London today. It was hard to let them go.

Stratford, November 18, 1597. The elms north of Swan Town have lost their yellow leaves by the bushel load. It's a sight filled with sadness too, another year passing away. I guess the world gets on with the fact of death by pushing through it, not letting it crush you in a heap on the ground. Yet I know in my heart that souls that truly love cannot truly die.

Stratford, November 21, 1597. I have been copying out some of Father's poetry on a particularly fine parchment he gave me. I like trying to imitate his handwriting. His letters arc and dip and wing across the pages like the swans on our river. They fly right to my heart.

Stratford, November 22, 1597. It's a funny thing when I pray: I hear no voices, see no visions. But I believe more when I pray than when I don't. Am I convincing myself? Or is God getting closer to me? But how could he be far away, when he is everywhere? Is he some kind of giant cobweb, that wherever we move, we tug one of his strings?

I just don't know. But I believe he is here right now, and when I pray, he listens to me.

Stratford, November 23, 1597. There is much whispering going on between Uncle Gilbert and Mother the last day or two. I suspect some plan is afoot, but I don't know what. Judith and I have been busy with our tasks, making butter, baking bread, and threshing wheat on the floor of the barn until we both look like scarecrows with all the straw and chaff in our hair, dresses, bodices, and shoes. Tonight, I hope to get a chance to work on my play again. I haven't been able to concentrate on it lately with everything that's been happening.

Stratford, November 27, 1597. I have actually finished my play, *The Parrot King*! Oh yes, a few lines still need some revising, but the basic play is complete, short as it is. Though my heart is still sorrowful over Grandfather's death, my fingers must do something.

My satire of the royal foolishness of this isle is wrapped in jests, puns, and indirection. It is no more than a shadow, but one that I hope will get people to thinking that fear is not something that was meant to be eaten with their daily bread and ale. And unlike Edmund's attempt at writing, there's not a papist anywhere in my play. So to speak. I can hardly wait.

Stratford, November 28, 1597. I am going to London! I was right, I sensed something going on. With Mother's permission, Uncle Gilbert is taking Judith and me to see Father. She said that it would do us good to leave Swan Town for a few days, and that a change of skies can give a heart some ease. I am so excited I can hardly sleep. We are planning to leave this Monday if the weather is clear, on three horses Uncle Gilbert has bartered the use of for two weeks.

I have written out my play on thin paper folded small enough to sew into the sleeve of my dress. And you, my journal, shall not miss out either. I shall sew leaves enough for you into my rose-embroidered bodice, close to the heart that gives you life.

How I would love to make a stop at Cambridge to see John, but I can't take that risk. So there's little I can do except hope that John happens to be visiting London at the same time I am. Yet it would take a miracle to meet him there without notice.

Stratford, November 29, 1597. Judith still can't believe we are going! As I have had to remind Mother, it will be my *second* visit to London. I am not all that green. And we have Uncle Gilbert to help us. I had no idea that the shop had done so well this year. The great heap of skins and leather goods he bartered for the use of our horses would have ransomed a princess. We leave for London tomorrow morning. Judith and I have picked out marvelous clothes for the trip. We shall each wear a fine cloak, of good woven wool, and dresses decorated with trimmed cuffs and collars of laurel leaves delicate as a spider's web. Uncle Richard has made us sturdy leather boots, with the shiniest buckles.

Judith is frightened of thieves on the roads. I told her not to worry. I also told her that I had finished writing *The Parrot King* and reminded her of what she promised shortly after I returned from London after rescuing Edmund.

"What? You mean you actually finished it?"

"Of course I did. How do you think I have managed to get through these days when Father has all but banished John from Swan Town? I had to do something! Anyway, you only asked me to stop writing plays that would incite a riot or enrage Tilney. My prologue is nothing like that. You'll see—it will be so much fun, and Father will be so proud of us. I just know it."

"Are you *sure* this will be all right?"

"Trust me. Everything will be fine."

"Well, I promised, and I'll do what I can to help. I just wish I could be as hopeful as you, Susanna."

"It looks to me like you're learning," I said with a smile.

Even though I am pleased that Judith didn't go back on her promise or tell Mother, I could hear more than a little fearful doubt in her voice. Dear sister! Have faith!

Later on, I also packed some costumes to wear if we get a chance to take the stage for a recital of my interlude. Father said he'd take us to the Globe, so we may have a chance to sneak onto the stage. The costumes are outlandish, especially the beaked mask for the Parrot King to wear. I've been racking my brain about whom I can get to play that role alongside us, but am not too worried. One thing I've learned about London is that it's a place where circumstances often take care of themselves in the most unexpected ways. I'll find my Parrot King somewhere in the Globe, that I know.

Stratford, November 30, 1597. We leave today. Though the sun is not yet up, the air is cool and the sky is clear, with stars as bright as I've ever seen. Our horses are both fine middle-aged mares with good dispositions. The weather for the start of our journey could not be better: cool mornings, warm afternoons with great mountains of puffy clouds filling the sky. We hope to cover almost twenty miles each day, then for a penny each get a room for Judith and me and one for Uncle Gilbert.

Somerset, December 2, 1597. There are so many strange creatures on the road to London. This afternoon, a beggarman, wrapped around with filthy rags, his left eye sagging as if someone had tried to claw it from his face, ran at us. He yelled like a beast in pain. "My young'ns, where are ye headin?" he asked. "Can you help a one struck by fortune's blackest hand?" He smelled worse than my uncles after a whole winter without a bath!

My horse rolled her eyes and stomped her foreleg in the dust when the man tried to grab my reins. Judith spurred her horse away and, with a frightened look on her face, watched as Uncle Gilbert approached the man.

"That's enough out of you," Uncle Gilbert said calmly. The wild man looked at him, spitting and drooling from his blistered lips. He then raised his fist and muttered threats and curses at me, of all people. Uncle Gilbert spurred his horse forward and struck the man a blow to the chest, knocking him to the ground.

"Come, Susanna . . . Judith . . . let this knave find others to practice his manners on," said Uncle Gilbert. I tugged my horse's reins, following Judith. Later, while falling asleep under our clean, cool sheets at the Broadside Inn, Judith told me that she had seen Uncle Gilbert throw the beggar a few pennies for a decent dinner.

Somewhere in Oxfordshire, December 3, 1597. I am so tired, I can hardly write. Every bone in my body aches. My feet ache. My toes ache. My legs ache. And oh, my bottom! But we are having a wonderful journey. Yesterday, the sky darkened in a second, and bolts of lightning stabbed down at the hills ahead. We crossed over a bridge and then took shelter in a large open-ended barn. Inside, several other travelers greeted us.

Even amid the muck and mire of cows and horses steaming in the damp air, we were grateful to be out of the rain.

Long Compton, December 4, 1597. The gently rolling hills of Oxfordshire are the most beautiful in the world. Well, the most beautiful I have ever seen. Clean sheets and a warm fire: what better way to end a day spent on a horse's back?

London, December 8, 1597. Our entrance to the city was a quiet one, greeted as we were by a soft, steady rain. Once past Uxbridge, we came in along a main road that brought us by Tyburn Hill, where buzzards feast on the tortured bodies of traitors (and martyrs, I might add). Despite being greeted by this sad spectacle, we are delighted to be in London. Judith can hardly believe we have finally arrived.

The open fields of St. Giles were beautiful even this time of year, and once we were past Newgate, the city itself was fabulous to behold. It was just as I remembered it. So many steeples! And people! Many from foreign lands, by the sound of their speech. Thousands fill the streets and alleys, jostling one another, singing songs, shouting, buying or delivering endless packages in every direction. And shouldering all this diversity of building and street and church, of course, the silver streaming Thames! Ancient houses line its banks, their gardens perfectly groomed. Though once we came within nosing distance of the river——oh, the foul smell! Our Avon is a river of paradise compared to the mighty, sewer-fed Thames.

There is so much here that it would take a lifetime to explore. But I must get to bed in this tavern where we are staying for the night (Gilbert doesn't know the city very well after sunset, and dusk is only minutes away), and tomorrow we go to see Father and the theater. I hope the audience is ready for *The Parrot King*. I know I am!

Five

" . . . I will play the Swan . . ."

London, December 9, 1597. We met Father and Edmund today and had more fun in one afternoon than in a month of feast days back in Swan Town. He promises us choice seats at the Globe. I can't wait! It's good to see Father in London, with all its churches and bursting playhouses. (It's also good not to have to worry about Edmund this visit, although my memories are full of thoughts of Grandfather.) Father knows the maze of streets here almost as well as his own plays. I swear there's a tragedy or comedy just waiting around each street corner and alleyway. No wonder he loves working here.

Father's new house is in Bishopsgate, about a mile from the Globe, north of the river, Gilbert says. There are all types of people in this parish, plus several rowdy inns that can each feed and lodge nearly three hundred people and their horses at once. Many inns have their own stages, such as the Black Bull, where Father said he first played upon the stage. While making our way to Father's, we nearly collided with three jesting players with drums and trumpet, announcing the latest showing at the Bull.

Of course, the first thing I noticed on our way here was the smell! I guess I was too preoccupied during my last visit to notice it, or it has gotten worse. Froth and scum! Winding alleys brewed the foulest winds imaginable, from flowing garbage and the waste of horses and such. Once inside Bishopsgate, however, things are a little cleaner. The streets are neatly kept, and the better inns filled with ballad singers and penny songsters regaling scores of well-heeled customers. Truly, it is a place where stages and players seem as necessary as bricks and ale!

London, December 10, 1597. This morning Father took us directly to the theater. Edmund had gone ahead of us, to make sure all the costumes and props were ready. Mist was still clearing from the riverbanks around Shoreditch, and the mud and the dung and the flies were everywhere. When we got to the river, we had to take a ferry to reach the Globe. The ferry by day wasn't so dramatic, I must admit, but Judith loved it.

Somehow, none of this mattered as we strolled into the theater. Walking into the pit, I felt dizzy as I looked up at the high gallery of seats that folded around us on every side. The great stage jutted out into the pit where we walked. I hadn't realized the players would be so close to the crowd. Yet as I craned my neck back, the sky—and a lone cloud or two sailing by—loomed into view. O Hell-kite! How do Father and his players keep their balance?

As Father showed us about, taking us now up into the high galleries, with their velvet cushions, then to where the tiring-house was as neatly organized and full of things as Grandfather's shop, I only pretended to listen. My mind was scheming on a way to get some players to help me perform my play during this afternoon's intermission.

Uncle Edmund has always bragged about a common player's ability to get his lines word-perfect in a matter of minutes if necessary, and today I wanted to put his boast to the test. As these thoughts were flying through my mind, Father began introducing us to his fellow players.

"Richard," he said, "you've already met my brother Gilbert. These are my daughters, Judith and Susanna."

A tall, somewhat portly fellow, with the most commanding eyes I have ever seen, bowed slightly, and after kindly greeting Judith and Uncle Gilbert, looked directly at me for an uncomfortably long amount of time. Taking my hand, he said: "I could pick you out of a whole city for your father's daughter, of that I would wager a day's takings. . . . By God, Will! She's right out of your left rib, she is!"

Father found this most amusing, and laughed until the top of his head turned red. I felt a little proud, but embarrassed too. I was so filled with awe of Burbage, the most famous player in all of London, that I could barely mumble a greeting. He must have thought me knocked in the head.

Father introduced the rest of the company to us in short order. They were all very kind, and seemed genuinely pleased to see us. One man in particular caught my eye: Robert Armin, the company's clown. He bowed with a courtesy that was both regal and very funny.

He told Judith and me that he knew over three hundred different dances, and twice as many songs. As if thinking we didn't believe him, he started singing a hodgepodge of them while his feet skipped the strangest dance I had ever seen. His Puckish face twisted into a dozen shapes a minute. Crafty rascal! Judith and I instantly loved him!

Somehow, in the whirl of events (the theater was rapidly filling for the afternoon's performance), Father took his leave of us, as he and the players had to get ready for the performance. A white flag—for comedy—was raised on the staff jutting high above the thatched part of the roof of the theater. Jester Armin was put in charge of taking Uncle Gilbert, Judith, and me to our seats in the galleries since he didn't have to be on the stage until the second act.

I decided he was *The Parrot King*'s only chance. If this wily jester couldn't find a way onto the stage, no one could.

For a moment, Judith's fear began to get the better of her. As we followed Armin and Uncle Gilbert, she began a whispered discourse about why we should forget the idea of getting on the stage. Oh poverty in wit! She was turning back into a shivering shadow of a girl!

I tried my best to calm her down, whispering over my shoulder.

"We'll be off that stage before half these sots realize we're even there, for goodness' sake!"

Judith didn't seem to take my encouragement to heart. But after clenching her fists a moment or two and looking very worried, she asked what we should do next. We'd just arrived at our seats, and I whispered directions in her ear.

While Judith distracted Uncle Gilbert, I cornered Armin.

Both his eyes started twitching anxiously as I outlined what I needed to do to get on the stage.

"Miss Shakespeare," he finally said, "am I to understand you aright that you mean me to steal one of your father's plays? Is that wot you're askin'?"

While he might have played a fool, Armin was far from witless. I had to think fast if this was going to work, even if it meant taking a few liberties with Father's name.

"Oh no, Mr. Armin, not at all. In fact, I already have it right here, a brief piece that my father penned himself. He asked me to see to it that it was performed as an interlude this afternoon."

"And what players are to be in it?"

"My sister Judith and I," I said somewhat doubtfully, knowing that women were about as common on the stage as horses and sheep, "and you, if you like. There's a part in it perfect for your talents."

"What! I'd be skinned alive for letting two girls on the stage."

"This bag of coins has a twin, Mr. Armin, if you could look the other way while my sister and I pull back our hair and put on our costumes . . . no one need ever find out, I promise." Even if it meant spending money earned over months of doing extra tasks, I had to risk it. There was no other way, and besides, the stage was so close I could touch it. Sprites and fires! I couldn't get this far and not get my play up on the same boards that my uncle and father played upon almost every day in a week.

"And Will—er, your father, is approving of this?"

"He said you were the man who could help us."

"He did, eh?"

"Most certainly."

"Well, that changes things a bit, for Master Will calls the shots around here, he does. Let me see this play sheet now, will you?"

I pulled the script out of my sleeve and handed it to him, along with a tiny bag of shillings. For a moment he said nothing. Then the jester scratched his head, chewed his lip a little, and blurted out:

"All right, Miss Shakespeare . . . I'll tell ye straight . . . we won't be able to put this interlude on today, no way in God's Heaven will we be able to do such a thing—"

"But my father promised me you'd help." I hated telling such a fib to anyone, but to be so close and fail seemed more than I could manage.

"Wot I was goin' to tell you, miss," he said with a smile, "is that today no such interlude can be played . . . on account of my needing to gain permission o' the prop master, but once I do that . . . well, I see no reason why we couldn't stage this short piece tomorrow. Then it's even a bigger draw, you see, for that's when your father's *Hamlet* goes on the stage for the first time, and there'll be hardly room for an extra hazelnut in this here theater, that I can assure ye."

"Are you sure the prop master will approve?"

"I don't see why not . . . he's my own brother, he is!"

London, December 11, 1597. Just as Father promised, he got us great seats in the upper left gallery for two performances. The one we saw yesterday was *The Merchant of Venice*. A story of a man who borrows money from some haunted creature named Shylock, and almost loses his life until a brave girl disguised as a judge makes a marvelous speech about the meaning of mercy. But all the while it ran on the busy stage below us, I couldn't stop thinking about the next day's performance, the tragedy of Prince Hamlet and the Parrot King. Would this jester come through for us?

As we walked into the Globe today, groundlings were already jostling in the muddy pit below. Some dancers, accompanied by a lutenist, were performing on the stage. The sky was overcast, with black clouds almost touching the Globe's towered peak.

I didn't see Armin anywhere. If *The Parrot King* was to make it to the stage today, it would have to be before *Hamlet* began. A play at the Globe was like unleashing a thunderstorm—once it started, there was no slowing down or stopping. That I knew. I clutched my bag of simple props, gave Judith a worried look, and followed Uncle Gilbert to our seats.

Just as we went up the steps to the gallery, a fight broke out in the pit. Bottles of ale were flying in the air. Curses and oaths bellowed out in accents I had never heard before. Maybe Judith was right, and this wasn't such a good idea after all. Would these louts even understand my play?

Goats and monkeys! This is *my* father's playhouse after all. A little prologue by Will Shakespeare's daughter shouldn't cause too much of a stir. Yet my heart beat faster, while the foul smell of ale rising from the pit seemed to grab at my throat, making it hard to swallow.

It was good at last to get to our seats in the gallery, and watch the blur of activity below us. But where was my jester? It took me months to write my prologue, and longer to save those shillings. An elbow suddenly nudged me square in the back. It was Armin, with a serious look on his face.

"If you and Miss Judith will come this way, I believe I can be of service to you," he said with a twitch.

Uncle Gilbert was laughing and drinking with some friends Father had introduced him to, and so Judith and I followed Armin down the gallery steps to the tiring-house without having to make any excuses. With all the noise, we could have sprouted wings and flown away and no one would have noticed.

Father and Edmund were somewhere behind the stage, getting ready for their performance. Perhaps they wouldn't even see *The Parrot King* at all. The thought hit me like an elbow in the stomach. How many times had I imagined their surprise as they watched my first performance in a London theater! It seemed terribly disappointing to think they would miss my well-timed shot at Her Majesty's pomposity, especially after everything we went through to rescue Edmund. But willy-nilly, my play had to go forward.

In a blur of silk costumes, whispered stage directions, and a whole medley of twitches from our jester accomplice, Judith and I stood with Armin waiting for *The Celebrated History of the Parrot King* to have its debut.

It was now or never.

Armin looked at me for a sign to begin. I took a big breath, hugged Judith, who was biting her lip and looking awfully pale, and nodded. We had rehearsed our lines last night, and I hoped Judith still remembered them. Before putting his giant parrot head on (he was playing the king, after all), Armin shouted to his left, "Awright, Buck, it's time—give us a blast of that trumpet, will ye?"

Even though I expected it, the sound of Buck's trumpet made me jump. On the other side of the curtain, the crowd immediately quieted. In less than a minute, the whole theater was still. I said a silent prayer, while my knees shook with a will of their own. The jester put on his parrot head, and then we stepped on the stage.

The huge raftered gallery and pit of the Globe came into view. Cobbler, tinker, baker, brewer, and who knows how many filthy butchers stood silently in front of us. Even with their dirty faces and humble clothes, they all wore a solemn look. Above them, in the galleries, sat the lawyers and doctors, the students at the Inns of Court, all robed in scarlet, ermine, and silk. They too were quiet, yet they seemed to be holding their breath to avoid contagion from the foul air arising from the pit.

I swallowed my fear, and began.

> "Gentles, I come before you,
>   Dressed in the finest feathers I could bring,
>   Knowing I present to you a tale of mirth,
>   A tale of our foolish king.
>   Hear now my tale
>   Wherein the Parrot King is scorned
>   Whereby the follies of our land
>   Are laughed at or more truly mourned."

Both Judith and I had pulled our hair back. Our robes were decorated with a hundred swan feathers dyed a deep parrot green. We must have looked silly enough. Mr. Armin was wearing the huge parrot head that I had made out of a broken well bucket I found in back of our house. His beak—fashioned out of scraps of leather and wood from Grandfather's shop— was nearly two feet long. His crown was a broken piss pot I had painted gold. He looked about as royal as a silly parrot could look.

The crowd was beginning to laugh at him, and he had not even spoken a line. I took confidence from this and continued with my speech:

> *"Whereat in this short prologue*
> *I do hope to show*
> *How one man's folly*
> *May keep a mighty kingdom's subjects low,*
> *Robbing them of their ancient faiths,*
> *Their freedoms to discourse as they see right.*
> *All echo the Parrot King*
> *So that their fortunes still shine bright."*

There now came from the pit a low murmuring sound. Their closely packed bodies began to jostle and fidget.

I looked to Judith to pick up her cue. Chaff and bran! After a pause, she began:

> *"And so I now proudly*
> *Introduce to one and all the Parrot King,*
> *A monarch who with his own*
> *Legendary lack of wit takes to wing*
> *And sets the tune that by the sword's point*
> *We all are forced to sing and sing and sing!"*

There were now shouts coming from the pit, but I couldn't make sense of them. Judith seemed to be gesturing with her eyes for me to look up. The sight was not reassuring. The entire upper gallery was standing up. Their furred robes formed a great semicircle of ermine and black silk and beards of various cut.

They were not smiling.

But I didn't have time to worry about that, for now it was Mr. Armin's turn. I could tell he was twitching from the way the parrot head jerked to the left every few seconds.

My Parrot King regally walked to the center of the stage and bowed to his subjects. Someone from the pit fired an empty ale bottle into the air that nearly hit Judith as it flew over the jester's head. Then, for a moment, the murmuring stopped, and we could hear Mr. Armin's throat clear as he started to speak:

> *"My beloved subjects*
> *In this richly blessed island of warriors and saints,*
> *The prospect of your thinking on your own*
> *Truly makes me faint,*
> *For what is this crown*
> *But a symbol of your monarch, father to you all.*
> *To shut the mouth and bend the knee*
> *Is required of every subject in this hall. . . ."*

Suddenly a voice cried out:

"These players here are mockin' our queen, they are!"

A great roar arose from the pit. The faces I had seen quiet with expectation now were twisted in anger, mouthing oaths aimed at us. Another ale bottle and some rotten fruit sailed through the air. I looked at Judith. Neither of us knew what to do. Mr. Armin, who couldn't hear very well through the giant bucket on his head, was unaware of the uproar we had created.

> "My gentle subjects, empty-headed drones,
>   One honest thought from you
>   Would toss your Parrot King right off his lofty
>   throne—"

"Treason!"

"Foul treason it is! These parrots must have flown in from France! Where else would they get such traitorous words?"

"Away . . . we'll have no traitors to Her Majesty here! Even if we ain't got a king, a queen's the same thing. Bess is not a parrot, I say!"

"Nor am I! Away with you! You puling cuckolds!"

"That's right, marry. None of us are parrots!"

And then, from the gallery, a booming voice suddenly yelled:

"Get these rank players off the stage, before the Master of Revels gets wind of this and shuts the whole theater down!"

The Globe erupted in chaos. With the pit writhing at our feet and the stern gallery glaring down at us, Judith and I seemed to have angered a monster with thousands of hands and eyes. Misbegotten clods! Where was my father? We had to get out of here, and fast. But where? And how?

"Get them!"

In an instant, the whole mob rose up and began climbing

onto the stage. The uproar had grown so large that even Mr. Armin heard it through his parrot mask. He didn't pause for a second, but threw his parrot head to the ground and ran for his life to the back of the stage.

"Come on, Judith! That's our cue!" The groundlings were barely twenty feet from us. They wanted blood.

After taking the same door that Mr. Armin went out, we were faced with a choice of going either up a stairway or down it. We both ran up the stairs, and burst into a room above the stage. After we bolted the door, our feeling of safety was short-lived. The room was the balcony above the stage. Not thirty feet away, the fur robes in the gallery eyed us and began yelling to the pit where we were.

"They're above the stage! Above the stage!"

"Break it down! They'll have us hanged if we don't take care of such traitorous cowards by ourselves!"

In no time, the door was broken off its hinges by heavy blows. I took Judith by the hand and pulled her out onto the balcony. There was no place else to go. We would have to face this crowd down or be thrown into the icy Thames. Or worse.

A motley crowd of men from the pit were already climbing the stage to try to reach us. The gallery suddenly stopped clearing out, and now they watched from their privileged places to see how our drama would reach its climax.

I grabbed a trumpet leaning in a corner and smashed it down on the head of a heavy lout who was about to climb over the balcony. Then, as the door crashed to the floor, I put the trumpet to my lips, and blew with all my might.

Unpredictable devils! The whole theater grew quiet.

Men and women seemed frozen in position by the blast of

the trumpet. It was the moment I had been waiting for. I tore off my feathered robe, pulled out the pin in my hair, and stood atop the balcony railing, some twenty feet above the stage. I took my second deep breath of the day.

"Stop! Listen to me! We didn't mean any harm! Treachery is the last thing on this earth we would ever think about, especially here, in our *father's theater!*"

This outburst stunned the crowd further. Men below us stopped climbing up the curtain, and the crowd in back of us halted in its tracks. Though one man held the parrot head on a stick and shook it in our direction, my words seemed to give them pause.

"Your father's theater?" said a voice in the gallery.

"Look, it's a girl!"

Someone hooted down in the pit.

"Yes! I'm Susanna Shakespeare, and this my sister, Judith. We are Will Shakespeare's daughters. You must believe us! We intended no harm to Her Majesty, may she be ever blessed! It's just that here, at our father's theater—"

"It's not your father's theater! It belongs to us, the Londoners of every stripe who visit here and make the Globe the success it is. Everyone knows that, girl," cried a voice from the gallery, full of scorn for my foolish presumption.

"That's right," said a man in the pit, one eye patched, his face red with anger, "and that silly play o' yours stands to get every one of us arrested for treason just watching it. Listen, everyone! I say let's drown 'em in the Thames."

The crowd surged. They were ready to seize us when I tried shouting them down once more. Judith cowered in the corner of the balcony. For once, I couldn't blame her. There was plenty to worry about now, and even standing high on the balcony, I already seemed to feel the cold water of the Thames closing around my throat. King of shadows! Where were Father and Edmund when we needed them?

Looking down, I saw an impish knave throwing hazelnuts at me from the stage. Whoreson dog! I had to do something.

"How can you call yourselves men if you live in fear of jokes, of jesters dressed as kings that never even existed? If you're afraid to hear a silly play, you're little more than base-born slaves! Or are you true-bred English men and women, worthy of enjoying this marvelous Globe?"

Another murmur spread now through the theater, this one suggesting that a monster was becoming a crowd, and then—I prayed—an audience. I drove home my point, realizing that if it failed, then all was lost, even if I had gotten the chance to perform my play.

"Don't make this theater a pit of fear, filled with men and women afraid of their own shadows. Bless this stage with your courage! Make it the one place on this whole island where our lives may be lifted up by the dreams of such men as Will Shakespeare."

"She's right! We shouldn't be afraid! She speaks a hogshead full of good sense, she does!" shouted a woman standing in the middle of the stage. When she met my eye, she winked and smiled the most beautiful gap-toothed smile I have ever seen.

"That's right . . . Will's daughters meant no harm . . . and that fool Robert Armin is probably halfway to Kent right now, he's so scared."

There was laughing now, and smiles all around. The many-armed monster had put down its weapons. A young man came out on the balcony and offered me his hand as I jumped down from the rail, a little light-headed from all the excitement. Judith now stood up and joined me. We looked out on the most incredible sight I have ever seen. The great Globe was actually applauding my speech, if not my play. I had won the heart of this wild place that celebrated or booed players and poets. And now even feathered monarchs!

Suddenly, a warm, rich voice from the gallery sounded in my ears.

"These girls meant no harm, that's plain enough. They're birds of a feather with their father, and that's no fable!"

That voice could belong to none other than John Hall! He was sitting in a sea of ermine. They must have been his fellow medical students and their professors, and they occupied nearly half the upper right gallery. And they were all smiling and nodding toward Judith and me, as if we had done them a great favor.

"Where were you when I needed you, John Hall? We were nearly driven to the Thames!"

"Susanna, you didn't need me at all, though I gladly would have come to your help if you had."

I felt my heart pound with joy and relief at the sight of John. It was wonderful to see him here, especially now after everything had taken a turn for the better.

But where was Father? And Edmund?

Judith tugged my sleeve. To our right, Father, Richard Burbage, and Edmund walked with quiet dignity onto the stage. They were in full dress, ready for the opening of Father's new play, which everyone seemed to have forgotten for a few minutes! Seeing them, the theater became totally silent. Father's voice rose up to the highest rafters and seemed to make the flag fly straighter as it waved from the peaked roof.

"My dear friends, please give these two clever parrots of mine the best seats in the house as you greet the Lord Chamberlain's Men with their newest and, I daresay, boldest play yet, *Hamlet, Prince of Denmark!*"

I have never had such a day in all my life, high above the playhouse's pit. King of codpieces! So much has happened that I can't possibly sort it all out now. I don't think there's enough paper in all of London for that. But first I must describe how Father's new play went.

He and Uncle Edmund were dazzling. Though Mr. Burbage was no doubt the leading player, the Shakespeares did quite well on the stage today. Edmund was the fiery Laertes. His swordplay made the audience shriek with fear and delight as he battled his way to a bloody end. (His pig bladder went off perfectly and drenched several groundlings.) I have never seen so convincing a stage death. Judith grabbed my arm and almost stood up with fright. His demise was even more realistic than Richard Burbage's. And Burbage was the noble Hamlet, the mysterious prince of sorrows!

Father played the ghost of Hamlet's father, the murdered king of Denmark. When he walked on the stage, clouds covered a patch of sun as if on cue, and the theater became almost as dark as the castle walls of Elsinore at midnight. His face was powdered deathly white and his voice was full of a painful longing I will never forget.

> "I am thy father's spirit;
>   Doomed for a certain term to walk the night,
>   And, for the day confined to waste in fires
>   Till the foul crimes done in my days of nature
>   Are burnt and purged away. . . . "

We were all as silent as any graveyard while he haunted the stage, an uneasy spirit on a tragic mission to avenge his own death and save his son.

On the way out, Judith and I met John coming down from the gallery. Zounds! Before I could get a word out, I gave John a long hug in the midst of the pit. How good it was to see him! In the excitement of the moment, I even invited him to join us at the Mermaid Tavern, where we had all planned to meet to celebrate this incredible day. Perhaps Father would see over a pint of ale that John didn't have horns on his head after all.

But John remembered my father's refusal, alas, too well!

"Thank you, but I had better not," he said wistfully. "After all that's happened today, I'm really not sure what to think. But I'm guessing we owe your father a little more time for him to see that I'm not some untrustworthy knave who's stealing his daughter."

"All this pretending is growing tiresome to me."

"It's not been any fun for me either, and I'm not half the player you are," said John with a squeeze of my hand. And then he was gone, lost in the jostling crowds of people leaving the theater.

Later. "Come here, my dear, and give this old bear a hug!" That's how Mr. Burbage greeted me at the tavern, in front of everyone, including all of Father's players. He was sitting before the fireplace. Burning logs crackled and popped, their embers drifting up the great chimney like fireflies. Singing, laughing, dancing, dicing, oaths flying, and ale foaming over gigantic flagons filled the place.

But when Mr. Burbage bellowed out his greeting to me, the whole tavern seemed to look up and listen. I was embarrassed, to be truthful. If the chimney hadn't been so hot, I might have tried to vanish up its huge maw. London's greatest player wanted to hug me?

"You weren't shy in front of our Globe, Susanna," said Father.

When I extended my hand for Mr. Burbage to shake, he stood and grabbed my arm and gave me a great hug. His belly was soft, but his arms were hard as oak. Burbage looked me in the eye and smiled so sweetly, it made me feel dizzy!

"What you did today, my dear, will never be forgotten by this troupe of players for as long as this great theater stands, that I can assure you! The crowds who come to our plays are sometimes forgetful of what we do for them, and it took a girl as pretty and as brave as a swan—mark you, Will, this girl is a regular swan, I tell you—to make them remember. I am forever in your debt, and at your most humble service." As he finished, he bowed before me as if I were the queen herself.

Just at that moment, when I was nearly swooning from all the smoke and noise and exciting praise from Mr. Burbage, John walked into the tavern! Trolls alive! What did he have in mind? I quietly made my way over to him.

"What are you doing here?" I asked.

John gestured for me to follow him out of earshot of my

father and Gilbert. Though both of them had seen John walk over to me, they drank their ale calmly and seemed more curious than alarmed at John's sudden entrance. Richard Burbage was in the middle of reciting a piece of poetry and captured their attention.

"Susanna, this may be the day we've been waiting for," John said once we were safely away.

"What are you talking about?" I said with a glance toward my father, Mr. Burbage, and the rest of the boisterous players. "You didn't think so an hour ago."

"As I was going to join my fellow students on their way back to Cambridge, I suddenly realized that after everything that's happened today, perhaps your father will relent and change his mind—I can't think of a better opportunity to at least try. This is our moment, I am sure!"

I looked into John's earnest, shining eyes, and knew he was right. This day had seen so many dramatic turns, why not one more? Perhaps Father would be softened by the joy of the hour to grant John's request to court me. In the roaring hubbub of the tavern, it was hard to think clearly. Yet when I looked over at Mr. Burbage, his arm around Father and his broad, handsome face filled with happiness, I saw our only hope not fifteen paces away, downing a flagon of ale.

"I've got it, John! We'll ask Mr. Burbage to ask Father to grant your request. I know how much Father respects him. He'll never be able to say no after you win that player's favor, I'm sure of it! And Burbage did say he was in my debt, after all."

John looked over in Mr. Burbage's direction. "You're right! Go to him! I'll be right behind you!"

Before I could even make my way toward Mr. Burbage, the

big player started stalking right in our direction, his deep voice roaring that he needed a piss pot and would be back to the tavern bar before anyone could down a boar-pig's bladder, whatever that was.

Zounds! Here was a now or never moment if there ever was one.

"If you please, Mr. Burbage, I have a request."

Mr. Burbage looked surprised.

"Yes, my dear?"

"Actually, my friend Mr. Hall has something he'd like to ask you." I had to hand this question over to John. Even in a tavern, courtly manners matter!

"Mr. Hall?" Mr. Burbage asked. He looked even more confused.

"Mr. Burbage," said John, "for some time now, I have wanted to court Susanna. Her father has once before denied my request. After the triumphs of this day, would you be so kind as to try to persuade him differently? We would be grateful to you for our entire lives."

Mr. Burbage's face beamed with mischievous pleasure, and his eyes shone with a brilliance that matched his powerful voice.

"And do you really love the girl? Love can fade as quickly as a flower without water if you neglect it."

"With all my heart I do, sir!" answered John.

"Though not exactly my type of role, I have always relished the character of Cupid. It would be my pleasure to help you, if I can, especially on such a day as this!"

Mr. Burbage turned around and bellowed out for everyone to hear:

"For God's sake, Will, get over here and bless these two lovebirds before they perish before our very eyes!" I had hoped for a more subtle intervention, but I couldn't complain.

Again, the whole tavern grew quiet. John grabbed my hand and held it tightly. Father looked his usual calm self as he walked over to us. He didn't seem surprised in the least. Did he know about my plans even before I did?

"By God, Richard, they do look faint with love," Father responded, after plucking a pint of ale from the tray of a nearby server.

"Do you mean you approve?" I asked, stunned.

"Yes!" said Father, his face beaming with delight. "John, some of my fellows have told me that as you watched Susanna's exploits this afternoon, and saw the crowd going against her, you quietly rallied a dozen of your friends to come to her defense had the crowd truly turned uglier. Sir, I am in *your* debt for such kindness, for both my daughters' sake. Though Susanna's acting skills made your courage unnecessary, I certainly took note. And I'm sure I'll come to terms with your Puritanism—someday! You may, John, if you wish, court my daughter Susanna."

"Mr. Shakespeare, I can never thank you enough! I shall strive to be true to your daughter always, with your blessing!"

"And you, my dear," said Father, turning to me. "I suspected you wouldn't let this kind man just slip away. But your mother and I weren't sure you were ready for this. Today, however, after the wit you showed in the theater, I have no doubt that you are ready for a proper courtship to begin."

"Hear, hear!" boomed Mr. Burbage, apparently forgetting about his need for a piss pot.

John suddenly reached for me with both hands and kissed me sweetly, much to the delight of the whole Mermaid Tavern.

"Could these days bring any more surprises?" I asked, my heart overflowing with joy. I even had to wipe away tears.

"Indeed, they can," said Edmund. "Go ahead, Gilbert, tell Susanna your news."

"Judith and I sent a rider to Stratford. Why, he's bound to get there, put your dear mother in his cart, by my troth, and have her here with us all in London in less than a week or Will's out five shillings straight, he is!"

London, December 16, 1597. Uncle Gilbert's rider was as good as his word. This afternoon, Mother arrived in London, courtesy of the hired cart paid for by Father. She was driven right up to the door of his house, with the City of London bustling and bartering behind and all around her.

"Isn't this a treat, now," said Mother. "All my loved ones within the walls of this great city. What have I done to be so lucky?"

Once inside, Father broke the good news of his approval for John to begin courting me.

"Somehow, I knew this trip would bring good tidings, I did. Susanna, I am so happy for you. I knew it would all work out in the end. I knew it as surely as we're all sitting here by this fire," Mother said.

"A swan always sings sweetest at the end," added Edmund, "and you should have seen Susanna sing before the Globe! Anne, you would have sworn she was born in that theater, and her sister too."

"Speaking of which," added Father, "we have a performance

within the hour. Why doesn't everyone rest this afternoon, and then join us for tomorrow's performance? I know the group of musicians who are playing before us tomorrow, and you'll enjoy them, I'm sure."

Father and Edmund left for the Globe shortly thereafter. John joined me and Judith at the market to buy some food while Mother rested. How good our fortune to be here with my family and the man who now courts me with my father's permission. All in the city full of people who are in awe of Father's theater. Tomorrow, Mother will get to see the great Globe for the first time.

London, December 17, 1597. And yet now I enter on the darkest chapter this journal has ever witnessed. God in heaven! We have yet to see its conclusion. Father and Edmund left to get ready for their performance. Crafty knaves! They wouldn't tell us what play they were going to put on.

John had joined us at the last minute after making arrangements to stay a few more days at Bishop's Inn, where he had been rooming with his student friends from Cambridge. Adam, his assistant, had come with him to London as an all-around servant, and he had to make sure the boy was kept out of trouble by giving him some errands to run. But now John was with us, on our way to yet another play!

The moment I saw the blue flag flying in the distance, I knew we were in for a tragedy. I pointed out the theater's huge walls and pointed peak for Mother. Though she had been to London before, she had never seen the new playhouse. She gazed at it with a look of recognition, as if meeting a friend of Father's she had heard much about but never met. We were ten minutes' walk away, and she was still mightily impressed. Just wait until she saw that stage! And the huge crowds gathered to see Father's plays!

The air blew coldly down the cobblestone streets as we walked by the various sellers and beggars and carts of produce and other goods. The sky had become a thick white blanket overnight, impenetrable to the eye. Here and there, however, a ray of pale sunlight broke through.

Soon we were across the street from the Globe. Its white-washed walls stood strong and high. Crowds milled around the entrance. Workers were moving barrels of ale off a large wagon and rolling them to the back door. Mother took all of this in with great pleasure. Here at last she was seeing what our father had dedicated his life to. How grand it was! I sensed that the sight of the theater eased the burden she had borne all those years without Father at home.

As we were about to enter the theater, I heard horses clattering down the stony street and the sound of a lashing whip. Half a dozen horses quickly encircled us. I could feel the hot breath of the beasts on my face, they were so close. Tall leather-clad men rode high in their saddles, with maces and pikes at the ready. The crowd scattered like mice.

"What on God's earth!" yelled John, pulling me and Judith and Mother closer to him. Gilbert reached for his blade but was quickly clubbed to the ground by one of the huge men. Judith screamed with sheer terror. The ring of horses parted, and flanked on the right and left by the villains was Sir Colin Hill! Dog-hearted harpy! I'd recognize that pocked, droopy face of his anywhere.

"Mistress Anne Shakespeare, under the authority of Stratford's council, I hereby arrest you on charges of treason, nonconformity, and suspicion of harboring priests—namely, one known by the name of Arthur Rogers, among other sundry and villainous aliases—all directly opposed to the laws of this most mighty of realms." One of the men reached forward, grabbing Mother's arm.

"No! You can't take her!" screamed Judith as she tried to push aside Sir Colin's men to get to Mother. Raising their iron maces, the stout men shoved her back into my arms as if she were no more than a sack of grain.

"Judith! You must let them go." I spoke quickly, my face close to her ear. Judith's tangled hair smelled of straw, of quiet country fields worlds away from this madness taking place in front of us. "Now is not the time to fight . . . later!" Even as I said this, my throat tightened with fear. This nightmare scene meant disaster, I knew only too well.

"No! They can't take her!" cried Judith.

John pushed Judith's hair back from her face and gently wiped the tears from her cheeks. I stood behind my sister, my hands on her still shaking shoulders.

John turned to face Sir Colin and his wart-faced followers. Mother stood imprisoned by three horses, walled in by black leather jerkins upon horseback.

"If you have any words to challenge this arrest, save them for the court," said Sir Colin. "This is what comes of treason— ye can't sow cockle and reap corn, ye know it as well as I."

"Master Hill, you know this arrest is groundless."

"Stay out of this . . . you know better, sir!"

"John—don't," pleaded Mother, her right hand extended toward us. "I'll be fine. This toad-spotted cur should fear for his own soul, not mine."

"Enough!" yelled Sir Colin.

"The Earl of Warwick shall hear of this," said John. "He's a patient of mine, and he cares deeply for me and my friends. I'm warning you, Sir Colin—don't do this."

"It might interest you to know that the earl you refer to was just this morning delivered certain charges for which he is to present himself to the Tower within the week or forfeit his estate," said Sir Colin as he tugged sharply on his horse's reins. "So you see, my friend, Her Majesty makes no discrimination. Treason is treason, whether it be committed by a lord or a commoner or the wife of a London player."

John was speechless at this shattering news. Judith buried her face in her hands, her body rocking back and forth with sobs. My heart broke as all the harsh words I had once tossed at Judith's fears came back to taunt me. Our worst nightmares had finally come true.

Mother's face was utterly calm, except for her eyes. They alone showed that she realized the peril that surrounded her.

"Pray for me, my loved ones. Tell your father what has happened. And how I love him," she said, her voice low but steady.

Sir Colin commanded his men to bind Mother's wrists. Their heavy boots scraped and shuffled on the muddy street as they flung her upon one of their horses. With a snap of a whip, Sir Colin, his men, and our mother vanished into the maze of streets, bound for Tyburn Hill and the same engines of torture that have sent so many to martyrdom. Mercy! The crowds around Father's theater had for the moment vanished. Fear had emptied the entire street. We were alone with the wind and the darkening sky.

For a moment, none of us knew what to do. The shock of seeing Sir Colin where we least expected him, and his arrest and violent carrying away of Mother, left us numb with surprise. Ripped broadsides advertising Father's *Hamlet* rolled past our feet in the breeze. Before long, people drifted back from side alleys and streets to the theater's main entrance, though only a few of them gave us a suspicious glance. We were in London, after all.

"That was some knock on the head, it was," said Gilbert as he tried to stand. John quickly came to his aid.

"No doubt," said John. "We should find a place for you to lie down, at least for a little while."

"Father should be inside the theater," I said. "Let's go in. We need to tell him what has happened. He's Mother's only hope."

We quickly made our way to the study Father had put together in the very top of the theater's tower, facing the river, clear on the other side of the theater. No wonder he hadn't heard Sir Colin's horses and Judith's screams.

I knocked only once, and in a flash he was at the open door, a long quill pen in his left hand. One look at our faces and he knew something was wrong.

Before any of us could say a word, a flock of pigeons flew off the roof into the air, their wings loudly fluttering as they hove out of view. Father's room had a huge window that looked over the rounded, open roof of the theater, and then out to the Thames.

"We have terrible, terrible news . . . Anne has been arrested," Gilbert said.

"She was taken by Sir Colin Hill and his men on charges of

treason, aiding priests, and nonconformity. Father . . . .what shall we do?" I cried.

"How in a hundred devils could they have found any evidence?" he asked. "There must be an informant in Stratford who's betrayed us."

I couldn't hold back my tears, and neither could Judith. Father put his arms around both of us.

"Now enough of this, my darlings. We'll never get Mother back by flooding the theater with tears. Gilbert, please sit down," he said. "I can see that Sir Colin's men have left their mark on you."

"He'll be fine," said John, examining Gilbert's wound. "He's had a hard knock, though."

"Don't worry about me. We've got to find Anne, we do," said Gilbert.

"How long ago did Sir Colin and his men leave?" asked Father.

"It wasn't ten minutes ago," answered Judith.

He reached into his desk, all cluttered with quills and papers and books, and pulled out a long object. It was round as a walking stick, but thicker, and had glass at either end of it. Was it a gun of some sort? What good could that do us now?

"This is a telescope," said Father, reading my mind, it seemed, "built by Humphrey Cole, who was an attendant at the Tower. In his spare time he made navigational tools. And we are certainly out to sea if we don't see where precisely your mother is being taken."

Father leaned out his high window and scanned the horizon toward the river. All I could see were hundreds of chimneys and church spires, St. Paul's in the distance, and the glint of the river where it peeked through a side street and caught the glare of the dull winter sun. There seemed to be a silence hanging in the air, full of expectation, and from the look of the sky, a heavy snow.

"Nothing yet . . . no, wait . . . there! I have them! Six black horses, not including Sir Colin's?"

"Yes, that's right," I said breathlessly.

"They've stayed this side of the river . . . wait . . . I've lost them . . . no . . . no, there they are . . . all right . . . I'd recognize that portcullis any day of the week . . . so we know the worst."

"What do you mean, the worst?" asked Judith.

"They've taken your mother to Newgate Prison. That's worrisome, since Newgate specializes in rapid sentencing and swifter punishments."

Seeing our faces darken, he quickly added, "That's also grounds for hope. She's near us, and we're very close to some influential friends of mine. They alone hold the key that will free your mother now. We must pray, and act with all possible swiftness if we are to save her. There's no sense running after her, though. Our written pleas of mercy must do their work now."

I hardly shared Father's hopefulness. Instead, I felt as if one of Sir Colin's horses had kicked me in the stomach. While I knew that the Earl of Southampton had saved Edmund once, Sir Colin's power seemed overwhelming. Where could we find the help necessary to overcome such a man?

London, December 18, 1597. Father has reassured us that Mother, while not out of danger, is still alive. His contacts in Newgate Prison have told him as much. Mother was being held in the North Yard, with more than a dozen commoners from Warwickshire. All were charged with treasonous practice of the old faith. There is much that can be done to win her release. But we have to move fast, as her trial could come at any time and without notice. Fortunately, Father has arranged for someone else in his troupe to take his place for the next several performances.

"What if we can't get her out? Sir Colin sounds so confident—he must have witnesses from Stratford. Mother won't stand a chance with the judges. They're not sparing priests, nor anyone refusing to acknowledge the queen's supremacy," said Judith, her eyes shadowed with worry.

Father got up from his chair, walked toward the fire, and stirred the logs within. After throwing more wood on the flames, he took out a book from a back row of shelves.

"What's that?" asked John.

"A list of important people," Father answered, "people who risk life and limb for their faith. I may as well tell you, for years now I have been helping priests and others of the old faith ferry back and forth from this city to Flanders. We've seeded this island with more secret priests than anyone will ever know."

We were speechless for a moment at this shocking news.

"Then you are a spy?" asked John.

"John!" I said. "How could you say that?"

"No, Susanna, it's quite all right. I am used to it by now," said Father. "And yes, John, I am a part of a secret network of people who are trying to preserve some flicker of the old faith on this island, some liberty of heart and mind. If you want to call us spies, well, so be it. I see it from a different angle, of course—more like a rescuer than anything else. Or a guardian of something very old and very precious."

"Does Mother know?" asked Judith.

"She has known everything, from the beginning."

"Doesn't this just mean that you too are at risk of arrest?" I cried.

"No, I don't think so. London is no Stratford. There are many lanes and alleys to hide in and many eyes to watch out for us. We blend into the city better than any floating fog bank, I think."

"And Susanna's mother . . . how can your friends help her?" asked John.

"Some of the information in this book," said Father, "lists the hundreds of houses in the city where fugitives from the crown can find refuge. Here too are some of the secret routes out of the country, to places in France and Flanders where one's faith is not a warrant for execution."

"That book could mean the death of hundreds," said John.

"It's written in a cipher that only a few know," Father answered, "and many of the key links are unwritten anywhere."

"How on earth is this supposed to help Mother?" I asked.

"Very good, my dear. You come right to the point," said Father. "If I can secure the help of the Earl of Southampton, he may be able to get your mother released from Newgate."

"Are you sure the earl will help us again?" I asked. "He's gotten us out of one crisis already. And rather unwillingly, I might add."

"The Earl of Southampton has helped me since my first days in London. As long as I wield a quill that can write plays and poetry, he'll help us, I am sure of it."

"And what of Sir Colin?" asked John.

"Sir Colin is a restless man. Where he's failed once, he most likely will try again. Therefore, once we get Mother out of Newgate, all of you must go to Flanders and live there."

"And what about you?" asked Judith.

"Oh, don't worry about me, my dear. I have ways to cross the channel at a moment's notice. When my days in the theater are done, then, Lord willing, I will join you permanently in freedom."

"But Stratford and Grandmother and our other uncles? Never to see any of them again?" I asked in a shaky voice.

"Well . . . well . . ." said Father, putting his hand on mine. "One thing at a time. Your mother must come first. There are worse things than exile, you know."

Later. Father has been out all afternoon trying to gain help for Mother. It has been snowing since early yesterday. The city is frosted over like a giant cake. Chimneys smoke, and steeples glare in the all-covering whiteness. We wait and pray.

London, December 19, 1597. Father is going to visit the Earl of Southampton tomorrow on behalf of Mother. Edmund has joined us. Though the Globe is closed because of the weather, he and Father are busy preparing several new plays for Her Majesty's court at Whitehall during the Christmas revels. Before the face of such a one! How do they do it?

London, December 20, 1597. The earl is nowhere to be found. Father is still confident. He says Southampton's ties to Her Majesty's privy council are strong. I pray his influence with the authorities in London is also enough to rescue Mother.

I wonder how she is doing, whether the prison is cold beyond endurance, if she is getting enough to eat. Today is so cold, the Thames is completely frozen over. Judith and I went out all afternoon, visiting the ice fairs on the frozen river. Hundreds of merchants and tradesmen set up shop right on the ice! Even their fires can't unsettle the solid white slab that joins this great city at the waist.

We have started buying treats for Mother on her return—a large basket filled with herbs from the Continent, packets of sweets and candies. But what I most want to give her is a hug that won't let go.

London, December 21, 1597. No news at all. I am haunted by what might happen. I can't stop thinking of the execution yard. The quartering table. The ripping knives. How they take your intestines out of you while you are *alive*, then throw them, before your own eyes, into a bucket of boiling pitch . . . fiends, not men, do such things, by Jeshu! When I told John about my fears later in the morning, he held me until I calmed down. He spends the evenings at Bishop's Inn, as is only proper. But how I hate to see him leave when darkness falls.

London, December 22, 1597. At last, Father has got in touch with the earl and has been assured that Mother will be freed by the end of the week! God's mercy! Our prayers have been heard! Perhaps news of *Hamlet*'s success reached the earl. After all, what powerful patron would want to disappoint a rising star like my father? John promptly rushed out to the market for some wine to celebrate the news.

London, December 23, 1597. This morning, Father shared with us the details of the plan for Mother's release from Newgate. The Earl of Southampton personally rode back from Somerset to meet with Father and send messengers to arrange Mother's release. According to Father, on the evening of the twenty-eighth, Mother should be cleared of all charges and released into our custody.

"Which gate can we expect her at?" asked Gilbert.

"The north gate, by the tidal pool," answered Father, now launching into his impersonation of the earl, all puffy with youthful self-importance, yet kind in his own way. "'Now, William, these royal favors don't come to me like leaves off a tree. Well, at least this time Bess listened to me, and so don't you worry about leaving the country or any such nonsense as that. That fellow Sir Colin Hill, I hear, has more hoarded grain than any man in Warwickshire. I mean to have some of my men pay him a visit, teach him how to respect a man's privacy.'"

I laughed so much my belly hurt. How good it is to be so close to getting our dear mother back.

Whitehall, December 24, 1597. Edmund has convinced me to join Father and him and their fellow players at the royal court for a performance they simply cannot cancel. Judith felt a slight fever coming on, so John decided to stay with her, and also make things ready for Mother's homecoming. Gilbert has gone to the local markets in search of items that can't be found in Swan Town.

I really didn't want to go, my mind was so much on Mother's suffering and her coming freedom. Players were the last thing on my mind. But Edmund was persuasive, as he always is.

"Susanna," he said, "you must come to the palace with us; there's really nothing to argue about. Your mother is coming home, of that we're sure. Your father and I and the rest of the players have a show to put on for Her Majesty's court. Come— you'll love it: the lights, the music, the royal chambers, it's magic, it really is."

"But what about Judith?" I asked.

"She'll be fine. Come on! If you liked the playhouse, you'll simply love the royal court!"

"How can I enjoy myself until Mother is freed?"

"I'm telling you how. Tomorrow you shall see the premier acting company of this entire country, and your father is the one to thank for that, you realize. And besides, we don't want the queen to not enjoy herself, do we? Will will do a better job knowing you're in the audience, as will I. Please . . . you can . . . you must . . . you . . . *will*!"

Switches and sticks! What could I say? No was simply out of the question, especially with dear Edmund doing the asking. I am so excited! In a few days, my mother is to be freed from prison, all charges cleared! And this evening I will see my father perform in his play A *Midsummer Night's Dream* before Her Majesty's court!

Before noon, almost twenty of us crossed the frozen river toward the palace, a sprawling collection of gardens and buildings now all draped in white. Mr. Heminges and Mr. Condell were very kind, and show in things little and large how much they respect my father.

Mr. Armin is still a regular laugh! As the company's all-serviceable fool, I think he sang every one of those three hundred songs he told us he knew! Though before he sang a single one, he said to me, "Never, never, never, never again ask Armin to open that door and allow you onto the stage, my dear. It's Pandora's box, full of mischief for the likes of you, it is. An' me as well!" With a laugh, I promised never to ask *him* for a way to the stage. But a pox on forevers! I had had an adventure to remember, that I know!

As our creaky cart full of costumes, props, and script books made its way slowly toward the royal residence, Father nudged my shoulder and told me to look back. Over in the south, the Globe stood in the blowing snow, a deserted giant, its hunched shoulders patient, waiting, I imagined, for my father's return.

Whitehall, December 25, 1597. Father and his company performed wonderfully in front of the royal court. The theater was lit by a thousand candles. Father played a duke who celebrates his marriage by having some unlearned, bumbling mechanicals perform a play of their own at the wedding. There are countless fairies in this magical tale, including Hamnet's favorite role, Puck. Edmund played a young lover hopelessly in love with the wrong lady, and he spoke his lines with great skill. He was right again! I am so glad I came. Celebrating with the Royal Court has been a feast for the eyes, and more—even we simple players got a chance to toast Christmas in high style!

The queen, powder-faced and plump, watched as if barely amused. Her dress must have weighed fifty pounds from all the jewels sewn into it. Father told us later that she personally informed him that the performance was one of the best she had ever seen. Perhaps the burdensome weight of those diamonds, emeralds, and sapphires makes smiling impossible!

Tomorrow, after we pack up all our props, we cross the river, and soon we will have Mother and freedom!

London, December 26, 1597. As we retraced our steps over the icy river, we were all in high spirits, singing songs. Freshly falling snow whipped and swirled in the wind, and Mr. Armin played his fiddle. As we bid our fellows good-bye, as well as Edmund, who was heading off to the theater, Father and I turned up Silver Street. I was bursting with stories to tell Judith about this special performance before the royal court. John had promised me he would be waiting for me with Judith, eager as she to hear how the play went, and my impressions of the queen.

As we walked into the main room, we saw Judith sitting before a smoldering fire, weeping as if the world were about to end. The house itself was undisturbed. What on earth could be wrong?

"Go away! Don't you see, any minute now, they'll be coming for you. Father, you must leave!" she cried.

"What are you talking about?" I asked. "And where is John?"

Before she could answer, a heavy pounding nearly shook the front door off its hinges. All of us stood still, frozen in fear.

"*Leave*, Father! Now!" cried Judith.

It was too late. In the next instant, the door was broken in, splinters of wood flying in the air as half a dozen armed soldiers moved into the room. Father quickly pulled out a rapier that was hidden behind the shutters, and pushed me out of the way before I could even ask what was happening. Judith wisely hid behind a tall pile of firewood in the far corner.

I had seen Father use a sword before, either on the stage or practicing for it, so I knew he could handle a blade, but this was the real thing! I stayed near the corridor leading to the back garden and watched in amazement as he took on six men at once.

He knocked down a bookcase near the table in the center of the room, creating a blockade with scores of books and the leaning bookcase on his left. Now the men could reach him only one at a time on his right. Father used this to his advantage brilliantly. He swiftly engaged the first man, thrusting and parrying with dizzying speed. He caught the man's arm while it was extending in a thrust, slammed him to the ground with his knee, and knocked him about the head with his rapier hilt. One down.

Another man filled his place. Again, Father's rapier flew about the man's upper body in a blur of speed. The man's two-edged sword was too slow to parry the lighter rapier, and the man fell when Father gave a powerful thrust to his right thigh. Two down.

The third man pulled out a cut-and-thrust sword that was lighter than the previous attacker's weapon and started to give Father some trouble. As I was looking for something, anything, to throw at the man, Father's rapier pierced his shoulder. The man dropped his sword, his face snarling in rage, and Father pushed him back onto the fourth man, causing both to fall to the ground in a heap of twisted leather jerkins and limbs.

Suddenly I felt someone grab me from behind. The back door! I couldn't see who held me, but I could smell the polished leather of his riding gear and the odor of a stable about him. I screamed when I felt the cold steel of his dagger touch my throat.

"That's enough, Mr. Shakespeare," said the man holding me tightly. "Drop it, or I'll cut her, I will."

Father's rapier clanged when it hit the floor.

"Don't harm her!" he said, panting for breath. "I won't fight you anymore."

The two remaining soldiers pulled themselves together and surrounded Father, pointing their razor-edged swords directly at his throat.

My captor shoved me aside and walked toward Father.

It was Sir Colin Hill! Again!

"Of course you won't, Mr. Shakespeare," he said with a grin on his pale face. "You have more sense than that."

"You have no right to come in here like this!" I shouted. Father took my hand in his, and the soldiers' swords retreated slightly, though they still pointed directly at us. Some of the men who had entered with Sir Colin helped up the wounded, while another pulled Judith out from the corner and shoved her toward Father and me.

"I have every right when a known traitor is hiding from the law, Miss Shakespeare."

"What proof do you have?" Father asked. "I am a member of the Lord Chamberlain's Men, not some masterless churl. On what evidence do you dare harass us?"

"What proof, you ask? Mr. Hall can best answer that," said Sir Colin.

"What are you talking about?" I asked.

"Mr. Hall has supplied us with all the information we need to arrest Mr. Shakespeare. Miss Shakespeare, didn't you know that many of your friend's patients who practiced the old faith have been arrested, no matter their age or their wealth? He has been a most useful informer."

His words stung my heart like fiery darts.

Could John have betrayed us? Could he help send to prison those whose lives he had been bound to heal? What hidden demons ruled such a man as this? Was this who I wanted to court me?

Sir Colin gestured to his men. They pushed me and Judith away, and quickly bound Father's hands behind his back and moved toward the door.

I began to grow dizzy. The room seemed to be sliding away from me. All I could see was Father's face and Sir Colin's cold eyes.

"What about our mother?" I asked. "She is to be released in two days, isn't she?"

"I shall not interfere with the earl's wishes; she will be freed. I am quite content to trade one Shakespeare for another, a minnow for the master pike behind so much treachery in this city. Mr. Shakespeare, I am well aware of the role you play in helping traitors escape the law of this land."

"The only role I play is on a stage, Sir Colin, and you know that."

"I know nothing of the kind, except that this game's almost finished, my friend, and you have lost," Sir Colin said coldly.

"Susanna, Judith, take your mother and leave this city. You must go, for my sake!" shouted Father as he was pushed out the door.

As the door slammed behind them, I sat down next to

Judith. Our father had been taken. Our world shattered. The man I thought I could trust with my life had just broken my heart with a single blow.

London, December 27, 1597. This morning I woke to a city clothed in white, while my heart knows nothing but darkness. My father imprisoned on charges of treason. And the man who has been courting me? My father's accuser before the law! Is this the same man who was ready to save my life before the entire Globe? How could John betray not only my father, but all those souls who trusted him as doctor, a healer of their pains?

Perhaps John never cared for me at all. Perhaps he only used me to get to my father, and his offers of courtship were simply a trap used to snatch Father from his perch in the theater. And so he has us both: my father imprisoned, and me betrayed.

But I must think of Mother now.

Tomorrow, before sunset, she is to be set free. At least that is some consolation. As always, Edmund was there at our darkest hour. He had come running with Gilbert from the theater the moment he heard news of Father's arrest.

"Edmund, he's gone!" I cried, nearly collapsing into his arms as he entered into the house.

"Don't give up, Susanna. We know by now, don't we? These things are not as dire as they sometimes seem," said Edmund, sitting down next to me, his kind gray eyes close to mine.

"Well, what are we to do?" fretted Judith. She was busy tending the fireplace, warming some dinner for Edmund.

"John has betrayed us all," I said, "of that I'm sure."

"I refuse to believe it," replied Edmund. "There's more here than we know."

"But he practically admitted it to Judith before he left."

"What did he say?" asked Gilbert.

"He told me to tell Father to leave the moment he walked in, and that he was very sorry, very sorry for it all," said Judith.

"Sir Colin told us everything," I said, my eyes filling with tears, "all we need to know. John is not the man we thought he was. He's a smiling, crafty, foul villain! A whoreson cur! A coward!"

Edmund put his arm around my shoulder and suddenly became quiet, as if some idea or plan had taken the very words from his mouth. But how could anyone help us now? My world seemed stuck inside some huge fog bank. Shadows menaced. Shapes shifted. Nothing was what it seemed to be.

"Thank you," Edmund said as Judith handed him some steaming broth. "First things first. When is Anne to be released?" he asked between sips.

"In two days at the north gate. At sunset," I replied.

"Right. Well, you two must be there for her . . . no matter what. As for John, I need to talk to him before drawing any conclusions."

"How can you say that?" I asked. "He has betrayed us, and me most of all! He's dead as far as I'm concerned."

"Susanna, the day is not over. I have some friends in this city too, people who just might be able to return your father to us . . . and John."

"Why would I want him back?"

"Because he still might just be the man you always thought he was, that's why. Now, Judith, can I have something more than just broth? I always want to eat like a bear before a performance!"

"But Father's in prison, not at the theater," said Judith.

"Indeed he is—but seeing that we're fresh out of rare old books, it just might take more than a little acting to get him out. I feel one of Susanna's now or never moments just waiting in the wings!"

London, December 28, 1597. Standing in the dirty snow darkened with garbage and every manner of filth, we waited outside the prison's north gate. The black maw of hell could not be more awful. Yet the setting sun briefly lit the streets and prison in a golden glow.

Judith, Gilbert, and I waited. And waited. And waited. Edmund had left us shortly after noon to try for Father's release. He seemed so hopeful. I half believed he would do it—and more. Yet still my heavy heart said otherwise.

Several of the city's poor huddled with us, as the high broad back of the prison sheltered us from the wind. Slowly the sunlight turned to scarlet. The rough-hewn stones of the prison wall blushed with their new-given hue. Nothing moved in the cold silence. Then a beggar suddenly began to sing a Christmas carol in a low yet clear voice.

> *"I saw a sweet, a seemly sight,*
> *A blissful bird, a blossom bright,*
> *That mourning made and mirth delight . . .*
> *O maiden mother's child,*
> *Sleep softty all this night. . . ."*

A crow squawked somewhere high above, and I briefly saw it dive into the swiftly gathering darkness.

Two tall figures suddenly moved near the gated door

about fifty paces ahead of us. Their halberds told us they were guards. I heard Judith catch her breath. Two shorter persons followed the guards, then passed them into the public yard. They began walking directly toward us.

One was certainly Mother! And the other?

Arm in arm, there they were! Our own dear mother and father! Striding toward us, Father's smile lighting up the darkness, that balding pate of his shining like a beacon!

Judith and I ran to them both, hugging and crying with more joy than we ever thought possible in this world.

Sprites and fires! Edmund had done it!

"My dear ones," said Mother, her voice catching with emotion, "how you must have worried!"

"We thought we'd lost you," I said, "first one, then the other. But tonight I know beyond doubt angels have watched over both of you, or this very hour would not have seen such a blessing."

"Angels—and earls," Mother said, handing me a small book with a soft, gilted-edged cover—Griffin's copy of *The Three Books of Life*.

"What are you doing with this?" I said.

"The Earl of Southampton secured our release because he wanted to," answered Father, "because he remembered how much a young girl from Stratford loved her family and would do anything for them. Behind that pompous exterior of his there's a heart of gold, I swear."

"I still don't understand. . . . I thought he valued this book more than anything in the world."

"There's a note in there for you," Mother said.

I opened the book, and sure enough there was a small, folded piece of paper, with my name on it. Opening it,

I read a smooth, flowing script:

To Miss Shakespeare:

This volume really belongs in your hands, as it has saved three lives so dear to you, and so lived up to its title. Remember always, no matter who you are or what you become, the greatest treasure in life is the ability to give oneself.

Yours,
Lord Henry Wriothesley,
Earl of Southampton

"What good can this book do me?" I asked. I questioned every kind act now. How could people give themselves to others when the world held such betrayers as John Hall?

Father put his hand to the side of my face gently, as he used to do when I was a child and needed him so. I embraced him and wept as I have never wept in all my life.

Later. Even as I was still in shock over John's betrayal, I knew I had reasons to be grateful. Not every day do people walk out of Newgate Prison after having been arrested for treason. Without the earl's generosity, my parents would be dead by now, and Edmund would have been lost to us long ago. So we have much to be thankful for. Gilbert and Judith were exhausted from all this racing about and worry and waiting. Once we arrived back at Father's, they both fell fast asleep, while I sat with my parents before a low, flickering fire.

As sad thoughts raced through my troubled mind, Mr. Armin suddenly burst through the door. The clever man with the animated face was not his usual self. He could barely get the words out.

"Master Will—Master Will—" he stuttered. "You will not believe it, Will, you won't—for all the b-blazing cups o' ale in the world you won't—he's here—and he's gone—that's fur sure."

"What? Speak slowly, Rob, so I can understand," said Father. Of course we were waiting for Edmund. Where was he? Gilbert had reminded us before going to bed that Edmund often spent long nights at the Mermaid Tavern. He thought he might be celebrating with some of his player friends and would see us in the morning.

"Who's gone? And who's here?" asked Mother. "What on earth are you talking about?"

"Sit down, Rob, and tell us, slowly," said Father as he poured a cup of ale to calm the jester's nerves.

"Well—it's like this—and well—it isn't—you see—I was coming back from the theater, to this very same neighborhood where we both live, by God, with more than half our troupe, and then I see there's one comin' here now—and then again—there's one—" The left side of Mr. Armin's face twitched three or four times. Then he sneezed.

"*Slowly*, Robert, as if you were memorizing your page from one of my prompt books," said Father.

The trembling jester took a quick drink of ale. Then he looked past Father, right at me.

"Oh, Miss Shakespeare—are you in fur it, to be sure—Master Hall isn't five minutes from this very house, or

I'm a busted crab, I am."

Branded villain! How could he come here?

"Is Edmund with him?" asked Father. "We are starting to worry."

Mr. Armin was silent. All his jests had vanished, it seemed. Suddenly, he got up and peered out one of the front windows with a strange sideways glance.

"Here he comes now, Master Will, here he comes," croaked the jester.

Was John going to finish the job? Have us all arrested? I made a dash to the front door.

There was a slight wind. I heard the muffled sounds of a horse galloping over snowy cobblestones and then I saw a torch, held by a man astride a horse. He was coming in our direction. Father and Mother, with the freshly wakened Judith and Gilbert behind them, came to the door, their faces full of concern for what this rider from the darkness might mean for us all.

By God! It *was* John! As his horse's breath steamed in the dark, he dismounted from the saddle, threw his torch into the snow, and grabbed my hand.

I flinched and tried to pull away. John would have none of it, but pulled me forcefully up the steps. His face was ruddy and he was out of breath. But he found the words.

"I know what you're thinking . . . all of you," he said. "I can explain."

"How could you," spat Judith, "after what you've done?"

"It's not what you're thinking—you must believe me," he said.

Father sat down wearily at the top of the steps. Mother

sat next to him and said something under her breath, a prayer, I think.

"Why should we believe you rather than Sir Colin?" Father asked with a calmer voice than I thought possible.

"Let him say his good-bye and take his leave," I said, my heart pounding in my chest. My legs felt as weak as straw.

"Susanna, I understand why you think as you do, but it's wrong. Sir Colin lied to you. He wanted your father to either leave the country or do something desperate and get himself arrested. He knew that to win, he had to separate us one way or another, so that's why he tried to implicate me in the arrest of your father—"

"And what about all those patients of yours who Sir Colin said were arrested?" I asked. "Just unlucky, I suppose?"

"Yes—I mean no. They weren't betrayed by me. They were betrayed by Adam, my young assistant."

"What?" asked Gilbert. "A mere boy?"

"Sir Colin bribed him," said John. "Adam was paid handsomely to provide the names of my patients who were at all involved with the old faith."

"Angels above—so young and so false?" said Mother.

"I am afraid so. So you see, I didn't betray your father. How could I? Nor any of you! Let God be my witness!"

Could it be that John was telling the truth? That he was the same man I once thought he was?

Judith was unconvinced. "Where is Edmund?" she asked. "Why isn't he back yet?"

"Yes, where is my brother?" asked Father.

"I am afraid, Mr. Shakespeare, that he is the reason you're standing here a free man," said John in an unsteady voice.

John's breath steamed as he spoke, curling upward to the starlit sky.

"What are you telling us?" I asked. "The Earl of Southampton ordered both Mother's and Father's release—we have his own note telling us just that."

"He did secure the release of your mother, but Sir Colin had obtained a secret order directly from the privy council demanding the death of 'one Shakespeare, the player from Stratford.' Edmund and I got this information from Adam. His suspicious absences led me to suspect something wasn't right. He admitted everything once Edmund and I sternly questioned him. The boy overheard all Sir Colin's plans, including his best efforts to strike both the theaters and the old faith with one blow by getting a royal order for your father's death. There was nothing the earl could do, unless he could make himself king, and besides, by the time he found out that your father was not released, it would be too late."

"He promised to help Father," I said under my breath.

"Some promises are beyond the best of earls," said Mother.

"Before I could make sense of this startling news, Edmund went to Sir Colin before your mother's release and your father's date with the gallows," John went on, "and spoke with him in private. He asked Sir Colin if for a certain price, wouldn't one Shakespeare player executed be as good as another. Sir Colin is down deep more of a zealot for cold cash than religious conformity or obedience to the queen. And so once he found Sir Colin's weakness, Edmund made him an offer of one hundred pounds if he would consider releasing William and putting his brother in his place."

"Where did Edmund get that kind of money?" I asked.

"His portion of the company receipts," whispered Father. "He was saving it so he could be a house sharer in the Globe . . . just like me."

Mother's eyes filled with tears.

"How do you know all this?" I asked. "If Edmund spoke with Sir Colin in private, then there weren't any witnesses."

"We met before he was taken off to the execution yard late in the afternoon. He said it was time for him to play the swan. Then he gave me this." John pulled a long quill pen from his sleeve. A swan's feather, delicately streaked with gray, like a sky at sunset.

London, December 30, 1597. So angels, earls, and actors have indeed watched over us. And now Edmund is gone. John also brought a letter from Edmund, all too brief:

My Dear Family,

All my life I have craved a role that would make the very stars hold their breath, marveling. I have found it. What joy I feel this hour, knowing you are safe. Tell Susanna there shall be music this day, on the river and in Heaven.

Yours,
Edmund

Sir Colin mercifully spared him the agony of quartering. In his death, my uncle has given us a light that shall never go out, come the darkest days. But was it supposed to end like this? Executed as a traitor, a man who would not betray his worst enemy for rivers of gold?

God's bread! The world is upside down.

Or is it? After John told us his wonderful and yet at the same time tragic news, we all took a walk down to the river together. My trust in him is restored, indeed, stronger than before. Father walked a little in front, and led us down to the wharves, where boats were locked in the frozen Thames. Across the river, the hundreds of sloping rooftops were frosted with ice and snow. Steeples stood tall in the clear night sky. Though Father said not a word about it, my *Parrot King* triumph now seemed such a foolish toy compared to Edmund's heroism.

Perhaps that was what the earl meant to suggest when he returned Griffin's book to me. By my troth! Maybe the most important work in this life is done off the stage, without theatrical flourishing, without that self-dramatizing, look-at-me quality that has guided so many of my steps. Not self-seeking, but self-giving, as the earl said in his letter. That was the key, or a least a great part of it.

As we walked back to Father's house, I suddenly realized that I had only just begun to understand Uncle Edmund's sacrifice. It will take a lifetime to really figure it out. But the fog had cleared. Father's fanciful works on the stage I will always marvel at, but Edmund's swan song is meant for a more lasting audience. One far above the rogues in the pit, or even the courtiers in their pillow-seated galleries.

And yet now, with a tragicomic ending worthy of the Globe itself, every good thought I once had of John is true again, and was never false. Is there a greater happiness? My poet father saved by a sainted uncle's bravery. John lost, and now found. Mongrel fortune! Such sweet sorrow, such painful joy!

London, December 31, 1597. Outside St. Saviour's Church the sunshine was brilliant but cold. For a player, Edmund Shakespeare had a lavish funeral. Filing solemnly into the church, all dressed in black robes, was the premier acting company in all of England. Among the more than a dozen players walked the famous Richard Burbage himself, followed by John Heminges, Henry Condell, and of course Jester Armin. John and I sat with Mother and Father and Judith in the front pew.

After the brief service, Father kissed the coffin that held the mortal remains of his brother and fellow player. He thanked his friends for coming, saying that times such as these remind us what stuff we are made of. Mother came out of the church with Father, holding his hand tightly.

As we all walked into the blinding sunlight, the great steeple bell began its tolling. Father had paid twenty shillings for Edmund's bell and burial service. And now, in the cold London air, surrounded by street criers, vendors, tradesmen, beggars, wenches, and market folk going back and forth along the winding streets, Edmund went to his final resting place amid the clanging, beckoning bells of the city he loved.

Father, to our surprise, let the jester have the final words as we stood beside Edmund's open grave.

"Men are giddy things," said Father. "They break hearts for pennies, they give the world away for love. Only those who become fools in the eyes of all can give voice to this mystery, a mystery in which I have lost a dear brother and regained the family I love. Robert, would you do us the honor?"

The jester answered with a twitch that seemed like a nod.

"I know it's not always me that's havin' the last words," he said, "but today is special, what with the kindness that Edmund showed us all, especially in these last days. And so, well, I don't know quite how to say this, being that someone else—*ahem*—is used to finding me the words, but Edmund knew that the script he was writin' meant his own death as surely as it meant our Will's life."

The slowly tolling bell high in the tower lent dignity to the jester's simple words. I noticed sunlight sparkling off the icicles hanging from the eaves of the great church. Their delicate beauty would have pleased Edmund.

"And so," continued Mr. Armin, "long after time sweeps away our dear, dear Globe, and the echoes of the laughter we've all raised up, and the tears we've wrung from 'em have stopped dry in their tracks, pardon me, Master Will, but after this stage is swept clean of us all, I daresay those angels in the sky above will continue to talk about what our fellow Edmund did this week, and they'll no doubt clink their half-pints of ale in honor of such a man."

"Hear, hear, Robert," said Burbage. "Well said! Now let's get us to the Mermaid Tavern, for I have some stories to tell of Edmund that need a crackling fire and a bowl of chestnuts to do them justice.

"Come, Will," he continued, putting his arm around

Father, "this sad day we'll sit down and tell stories of players who should be kings and let your brother's bravery flower into some of the greatest plays this city has ever seen. He was a gifted player, that he was, quite a stalk from the Shakespeare family tree." Then, with a wink in my direction, he added, "Much the same spirit as that daughter of yours, Will! By God, much the same, I tell you!"

While everyone drifted away from the church, Father took me aside for a minute. His eyes seemed to see right through me.

"After all that we have been through, my dear, I want you to know how proud I am of you. Burbage is right. Your now or never spirit is what makes you the special swan you are, and that gift you must never lose!"

I gave him a great hug, and we joined the others. Father knew that the next day we would have to depart for Swan Town. He would say good-bye in the morning. In honor of Edmund, Mother and Gilbert joined him at the tavern, yet John and I returned with Judith to Father's house. A boisterous tavern wasn't the place I wanted to be today.

"I keep thinking of the story you told me about that spot in the Avon's currents, pulled back by a miracle of love," said John as we walked down the busy London street. "We must count our days aright, after what Edmund has done for us."

Old Maggie with her chicken blood wasn't far off after all. A brother for a new son. And John was true all along, as true as Edmund was generous. Queen of curds and cream! How could I have doubted him?

London, January 1, 1598. Shortly after sunrise, Father walked with us for a few minutes on our way to the Oxford road leading homeward. He arranged a cart for Mother, Judith, and me, while John and Gilbert rode by our side. John would soon turn from us to pick up the road to Cambridge and his further studies, though with our courtship approved, he promised to visit as often as possible. The city itself was still sleeping. Here and there, a few men washed down the streets in front of their shops. A distant church bell rang, muffled by the thick morning air.

Father held Mother close as he kissed her good-bye.

"It's time, my dears, for us to part again," he said, walking briskly alongside our cart, his eyes brightening with each word. "The days we have seen would break any heart not made of stone, I am sure, but the Earl of Southampton has assured me that he will do all he can to help those Sir Colin has arrested. So there's no need, young Hall, to worry overmuch. Now, Anne, you look after my gardens, and watch for the canker in the spring roses. There's nothing worse. And Gilbert, you keep that shop in busy form, for our company will come calling again for your handcrafted goods, I have no doubt! I am going to miss all of you, my dear ones! I will visit you soon, I promise. Here in this town of steeples, not a bell will toll but I will pray for you all, my swans, my heart's delight. And you, John Hall, I want no reports of sickness unattended. Now mind you, get those herb gardens going in the spring. An early start is the shortest way to a long harvest. Keep your uncle Edmund in your prayers. He will watch over you still. There's nothing surer in this feverish world."

Father went on like this for nearly a mile. Finally, he shook hands with John and Gilbert, turned to us and bowed, and started his walk back. I turned in my seat and watched him until he was swallowed up by the crowds and towers of the now-awakened city.

1616 April 25 Will. Shakspere, gent{leman}.
—Stratford Burial Register

HERE LYETH YE BODY OF JOHN HALL,
GENT{LEMAN}: HE MARR{IED}: SUSANNA,
YE DAUGHTER {AND COHEIRE}
OF WILL SHAKESPEARE, GENT{LEMAN}.
HEE DECEASED NOVE{EMBER} 25, A. 1625
—Burial Inscription, Holy Trinity Church, Stratford

WITTY ABOVE HER SEXE, BUT THAT'S NOT ALL . . .
WISE TO SALVATION . . .
SOMETHING OF SHAKESPEARE WAS IN THAT . . .
11 JULY, 1649.
—Susanna Shakespeare Hall's Burial Inscription,
Holy Trinity Church, Stratford

Author's Note

Susanna's Story

On her gravestone inscription at Stratford, Susanna Shakespeare has the distinction of being the only child of the famous playwright publicly compared to her father. What they had in common, not surprisingly, was intelligence, or as people of Shakespeare's time would have said, wit.

This story is the result of my imagining just how life might have been for Susanna and her family. While trying to be faithful to many historical details of the period, I have nevertheless invented most of this story. But Susanna was an actual person, and her struggles were no less real than our own.

Though Susanna's life in Stratford lacked the modern conveniences we take for granted, being the daughter of England's greatest writer surely provided more than a little excitement. True, playwrights in Shakespeare's time weren't glamorous celebrities. But William Shakespeare was indeed her father, and her closeness to him would have provided her with a unique perspective on his character and personality.

Shakespeare's Family
and Theater

William Shakespeare married Anne Hathaway in November 1582. He was eighteen years old, while his bride was seven or eight years his senior. On May 26, 1583, Susanna, their first child, was born. The baptismal record for 1585 at Stratford records the baptism of Hamnet and Judith Shakespeare on February 2. The twins were named after Hamnet and Judith Sadler, residents of Stratford who were fined at least once for not attending the established worship services at Holy Trinity Church. Hamnet Shakespeare died of unknown causes and was buried on August 11, 1597. Judith married Thomas Quiney (sometimes spelled Quyny) of Stratford only months before her father died in 1616. She lived to be seventy-seven years old. Susanna actually married John Hall in 1607. She died in 1649, sixty-six years old.

From shortly after the birth of Shakespeare's twins, the record of Shakespeare's whereabouts is a blank until the early 1590s, when he appears as an aspiring poet and playwright in London. While some biographers have claimed that Shakespeare "abandoned" his wife and family for the London stage, there is no solid evidence for this. In fact, his wife, Anne, upon her death in 1623 at age sixty-seven, was buried beside her husband inside Trinity Church. Abandoned wives are not commonly buried beside their renegade husbands.

Because the Globe theater is so identified with

Shakespeare, I have moved the date of its construction back a year or so in order to give Susanna and her sister a chance to visit it in my story. The real Globe theater opened in 1599, and actually burned down during a performance in 1613, though it was quickly rebuilt afterward. I have also moved the traditional dating of Shakespeare's *Hamlet* by two years, partly for storytelling purposes and partly because I agree with Professor Harold Bloom that Shakespeare probably revised *Hamlet* through the 1590s. In any event, a compression of actual history here and elsewhere has helped me bring more drama to Susanna's journal than I would otherwise have by following strict historical chronology.

Shakespeare's Religion

The religious situation in England in the second half of the sixteenth century was a complicated one. There were basically two major groups: the Roman Catholics and what we now call the Protestants. The first acknowledged the pope as the supreme authority in faith and morals, and its practice (the "old faith") was forbidden during Queen Elizabeth's reign. The second group was more varied in belief, ranging from Anglicans, who affirmed Elizabeth I as supreme head of the Church of England (the "established church"), to the Puritans, who often saw no authority higher than the local congregation. It was the Puritans who vigorously opposed the public theaters in Shakespeare's time and characterized them as magnets for vice.

Amid all the speculation about Shakespeare's religion, we know for sure that in 1757, carpenters found a Catholic "spiritual testament" hidden in the house of his father, John Shakespeare. In 1580 the Jesuit Edmund Campion passed through the English midlands, once even staying near the north of Stratford handing out similar spiritual literature. Catholics who wished to privately swear allegiance to the "old faith" signed documents called spiritual testaments and then hid them in their houses as private proof of their adherence to an outlawed faith.

John Shakespeare's testament has all the marks of a genuine document. It suggests a world of secret prayers, of hidden faith, and of sporadic persecutions, during a time when religious freedoms were still largely unknown. Practicing the Catholic faith was punishable by heavy fines. A priest caught preaching or saying mass faced torture and death by quartering. This was Edmund Campion's fate in 1581.

In 1606, and again shortly after her marriage to Dr. Hall, Susanna Shakespeare's name appears on a list of Stratford citizens fined for not attending Holy Trinity church. Catholics often refused to attend established services out of conscience, even in the face of financial ruin. John Shakespeare appears on such a list in the early 1590s, though there is some evidence that he might have been avoiding church to elude arrest for debt. Susanna's nonattendance suggests more spiritual motives.

William Shakespeare now is something of an industry, a subject to be studied in school, college, and university. In addition to being a successful playwright, he was also a husband and a father, and just as preoccupied with the worries of everyday living—such as the price of land, the reputation of his family, and the happiness of his daughters—as anyone else.

Out of such stuff his dreams were made, for his Globe and ours.